D1267891

Hugo von Hofmannsthal

Hugo von Hofmannsthal
three plays

Death and the Fool

Electra

The Tower (1927)

Translated with an introduction by
Alfred Schwarz

WAYNE STATE UNIVERSITY

Wayne State University Press, Detroit, 1966

To the memory of my father

contents

acknowledgments

MY WORK ON these translations was initially made possible by a fellowship from the Council of the Humanities, Princeton University. I am grateful to several readers who saw different parts of the manuscript. My special thanks go to Michael Hamburger for his suggestions toward improving the translation of *Electra* and to Eric Bentley for his encouraging interest in my version of *The Tower*.

Part of the Introduction was first printed in the *Tulane Drama Review*, IV, No. 3 (Spring, 1960), copyright © 1960. The authorized English translations of the three works of Hugo von Hofmannsthal here included vest exclusively in Bollingen Foundation, New York. Their permission to publish my translations of *Tor und Tod* and *Der Turm* (1927) is gratefully acknowledged. My translation of *Elektra* is reprinted by permission from *Selected Plays and Libretti*, Volume 3 of Selected Writings of Hugo von Hofmannsthal, published by Bollingen Foundation.

Finally, I am indebted to the standard critical commentaries on Hofmannsthal, particularly those of Ernst Robert Curtius, Karl J. Naef, and Grete Schaeder.

A. S.

biographical note

HUGO VON HOFMANNSTHAL was born in Vienna in 1874. His earliest work appeared under the pen name of "Loris" and gained him considerable fame before the age of twenty. He studied romance philology at the University, but meanwhile produced poems, stories, essays, reviews, and the short lyric dramas (*The Death of Titian, Death and the Fool, The Little Theater of the World*, among others) before the turn of the century. He married in 1901 and lived in Rodaun, in the neighborhood of Vienna, for the rest of his life. The fortunate results of his collaboration with Richard Strauss are well known. He was a librettist of high distinction. Aside from *Electra*, a drama which later served Strauss as text for his opera, he wrote *The Cavalier of the Rose* (1911), *Ariadne in Naxos* (1912, 1916), *The Woman Without a Shadow* (1919), *The Egyptian Helena* (1928), and *Arabella* (1933). These were produced as operas, yet each libretto is a work of dramatic art in its own right. Besides the dramas on Greek subjects, mentioned in the introduction to this book, Hofmannsthal wrote a version of *Alcestis* and of *King Oedipus* which Max Reinhardt produced in 1909. His genius for comedy is best exemplified by *The Difficult Man* (1921). Reinhardt also persuaded him to write a new version of *The Tower* for the theater (1927) which is the one included in this volume; it was his last great dramatic work. He died in 1929 at Rodaun. Hofmannsthal's voluminous work has been

11

collected in a recent edition by Herbert Steiner. An excellent short selection of his poems, plays, tales, and literary essays is available in two volumes, edited by Rudolf Hirsch (Frankfurt a. M.: S. Fischer Verlag, 1957).

introduction

I

IN THE YEARS since World War II Hofmannsthal has been
regaining the recognition of his authority in modern letters.
As the persistent image of the precocious poet-esthete of the
1890's, the "neo-romantic" impressionist poet of the literary
histories, receded, or rather fell into proper place, we have
been rediscovering in his later work a contemporary writer
of impressive stature. As Ernst Robert Curtius pointed out in
the memorial essay of 1929, the year of Hofmannsthal's
death, his authority was that of responsible and representative authorship in a critical time; authority in the sense of
jurisdiction and testimony, the exercise of an historic trust.
All his writing bears witness to his constant sense of the
magisterial meaning of the word *author*.

But it has always been in the theater that such authority
made itself practically and most immediately felt. The potential author for a moment steps out of the undefined crowd of
spectators, his community audience, and becomes the representative actor. His function is most serious when he poses as
comic or tragic actor on a universal stage. Hofmannsthal's
career as a playwright is the record of his effort to revitalize
the great tradition of European drama on the modern stage.
He tried in several ways to re-establish the authority of a
truly representative theater.

13

His dramatic experiments and critical reflections con-
stitute a highly instructive syllabus of the problems involved
in trying to transform the modern stage into a vital and representative theater. The theater was once and could again
become, so he thought, the showplace of the individual and
the collective conscience, of the inner as well as the outer life
of a people. Shortly after the first world war, he began to
publicize his idea of a popular festival theater in Salzburg, a
theater for music and drama, where the life of a culture may
momentarily take its characteristic shape. This might be in
the form of a folk drama, a simple medieval morality, or the
sophisticated art of Mozart; he argued persuasively that the
repertory would uncover their basic kinship. The first production on that stage was Hofmannsthal's modern *Everyman*, his revival and adaptation of the medieval morality.[1]

The play had been published in 1911; it was Reinhardt's
idea to inaugurate the Salzburg festivals with its presentation
on the cathedral square. The annual staging of the Salzburg
Jedermann is still a central attraction at the festivals. Its
initial success must have been especially gratifying since it
promised to re-establish the theater as a communal institution.
It reawakened in the local spectators an immemorial tradition,
said Hofmannsthal, the natural popular impulse toward public representation and performance. And it proved what he
had suspected, that certain traditional dramatic subjects were
durable and lively in a new context.

The production outdoors on the *Domplatz* seems to
have been something of a revelation. A scaffold which ap-
proximated the plan of the late medieval English stage faced
the crowd of spectators, and upon it the story of Everyman
was projected. The simple action unfolded in the multiple
language of theater—gesture, ceremony, music, and dance—
which these people understood at once. Hofmannsthal's account of the first performance emphasizes the impressiveness
and at the same time the naturalness of the scene in front of

the cathedral, the sense simultaneously of awe and familiarity in the audience. Here is a paraphrase of his description:

First, the flourish of trumpets, and the *nuntius* or prolog stood quite naturally against this background. Familiar and appropriate was the effect of the tall marble saints between which the actors appeared and disappeared; startling and yet not strange, the call of "Jedermann" from the towers of the church nearby, down from the fortress, and from the church-yard of St. Peter. The great bells boomed forth at the end of the play, and the six angels moved into the twilight of the portals, while the Franciscan monks watched the spectacle from their tower and the priests from the hundred windows of the convent of St. Peter. In this setting, the whole performance, tragic, comic, symbolic, seemed self-evident. There was nothing strange or alien in all this for the peasants who streamed into the town, first from the outskirts, then from nearby villages, and finally from greater and greater distances. They spread the word: the players are back again; that's as it ought to be.[2]

The tone of Hofmannsthal's report of this occasion, as indeed of all his prose writings on the social function of the theater, is noticeably high-spirited. He viewed the theater in terms of its intermittent and ideal function in society. Therefore, ignoring the modern renascence of the drama since Hebbel and Ibsen, he turned deliberately to the past for his idea of a theater. The last phrase of his account—*"Es wird wieder Theater gespielt. Das ist recht"*—directs our attention to the long tradition of theatrical performance in the communities of Europe; that is to say, the theater as these people had traditionally known it has come to life again, the mirror of things visible and invisible. Its religious and social function, as he outlined it, has always been the same: they arrive as individual spectators, but as they gather before the scaffold or the stage they merge into the common crowd; they become the chorus. And as the actor steps out upon the boards, he becomes the representative of all, in front of mankind, for mankind. In his virtual action on this universal stage he figures the suffering of the others; for them he carries on the litigation with God and with the time. This, Hofmannsthal observed, has been the age-old formula from *The Persians* of Aeschylus until today.[3] The paradoxical situation of the actor on such a stage is remarkably effective; for he stands apart from the crowd, perhaps even in conflict with it, possibly marked as an outcast, and yet he represents each individual essentially. He is still "the mask of the god, the character who suffers for the others."

Hofmannsthal's account of the successful production of his modern *Everyman* virtually celebrated the realization of such a conception of theater. He found that his imagination demanded a symbolic stage, a theater like the medieval-Elizabethan or Calderón's; and in turn such a conception of playing the great world drama, as it were, under the eyes of God demanded the allegorical mode. Reaching back in the European tradition, he revived a Catholic world theater in the baroque style. His subsequent production, *The Salzburg Great Theater of the World*, exemplified the timeliness of such a drama as well as its long, "metaphysical" perspective.[4] It is a drama which bypasses the uses of psychological realism because it theatricizes the typical situation, not individualized character. It enacts before us the impalpable life of the soul; it tests the creature under the eyes of the creator. And though there is no prolog in heaven at the beginning of *The Tower*, yet the dramatic conception is the same.

"Situations are symbolic," Hofmannsthal remarks in the *Book of Friends;* "it is the weakness of our time that we treat them analytically and in so doing dissolve the magic."[5] And elsewhere: the "magic," the real "mysterium of Nature" escapes the naturalistic mode of imitation. For it projects "an impalpable life upon a very arbitrarily chosen social plane.

16

The maximum of the human personality . . . cannot be caught naturalistically."

But there have always been nostalgic arguments against the possibility of a modern tragic theater which is frankly metaphysical in nature. Supposedly tragedy has fled the modern world since the dignity of man and his traditional values are gone. In 1926, in the most intelligent formulation of these arguments, I. A. Richards (in *Science and Poetry*) described "the transference from the Magical View of the world to the scientific" which entailed a drastic reorganization of our attitudes. If the contemporary poet cannot confront or chooses to evade the changed world-picture, Richards concludes, he runs the risk of being obsolete in his own lifetime. But the modern poetic dramatists, like Hofmannsthal, Yeats, Claudel, and Eliot, neglect this confrontation in their work not merely from personal conviction, but also for artistic reasons. The scientific-naturalistic view of the human condition strikes them as being an unwarranted reduction of what they perceive in the human personality. Theirs is a minority voice because the modern Everyman simply does not care to be fully represented; he does not care to confess either his significance or his insignificance. And the naturalist theater which he patronizes respects the proscenium arch; it keeps him forever and safely the spectator. It speaks seldom to him individually *of* himself, but rather to him generally *about* those like himself. The missing fourth wall makes fewer demands upon him than the concave mirror. That is why Hofmannsthal found no use for the social premises and the conventions of the realistic and naturalistic drama at a time when it reigned supreme on the European stages. If he chose not to betray himself and his audience with impressive shadow play, his alternatives were silence or the difficult attempt at creating a new, vital theater in order to regain the scope of the great theaters of the past.

Thus he experimented continually with traditional dramatic subjects; for he knew that true subjects, those which have permanent significance, are rarely found, and that the modern playwright, in his search for subject, has a natural and lasting obligation to the tradition. For him it was an obligation in both senses of the word: a duty towards it to keep that which is true and valid actively alive, and an indebtedness to it for its creative and operative qualities in a new context. For the purposes of art such subjects are virtually inexhaustible. Hofmannsthal recognized that the animating quality of tried dramatic subjects, that which rendered them durable and lively, was that they represented action (*Handlung*), not event (*Geschehen*). He spoke of action as symbolized event, the necessary, not the accidental, manifestation in doing or suffering; that is to say, action is an event which is not adventitiously imposed upon the characters, but renders their potential existence and function actual. Shakespeare, for example, turned event almost always into action. Such drama remains alive in that it re-creates itself with each reconsideration. To the artist who searches for subject, the tradition is thus self-perpetuating and forever new ground. At the height of his powers he *recognizes* living subject when he sees it, for he has it already potentially in him as a perceptive representative of his time.

In comparison with the starkly realistic social and psychological dramas of his day, Hofmannsthal's work appears to have an old-fashioned, strongly literary flavor. He revived the figures of the ancient Greek drama and the Christian allegories, and brought them back on the modern stage. As in T. S. Eliot's first plays, written before he rediscovered the drawing-room comedy as a way of concealing his sterner purposes, Hofmannsthal re-dramatized ancient subjects and asserted his orthodox Christian reading of the human condition in traditional theatrical forms. For man's precarious

18

estate in this world has not changed. We exist still narrowly confined and in darkness, he wrote in an essay on his *Everyman;* our eyes look farther and deeper, yet the inner eye is weak. Much is at our disposal, yet we cannot dispose; what we ought to possess, possesses us. The subject is timeless and humanly absolute, an allegory valid today as centuries ago. "It is the risk and the glory of our time, the aged Ibsen standing on its threshold, that we have again come far enough to have to prove ourselves in allegory." This was written in 1912.[6] He had discovered the roots of his modern theater.

In fact, the entire evolution of Hofmannsthal's tragic theater can be understood as one comprehensive allegorical vision of man's pilgrimage on earth. It is in a sense a confessional drama which mirrors a creative spirit moving from pre-existential, pre-tragic experiences through life as tragic choice, the problem of human action, to a final image of transcendence or deliverance. The structure of this mammoth drama of a lifetime has three discernible stages. Chronologically, there are first the lyric playlets of the last decade before the turn of the century; then, in the years preceding the first world war, a period of search and experimentation, a wrestling with larger dramatic structures, the attempt to discover a theater of significant action for the times; and after the major catastrophe of the war until his death in 1929, years of personal restlessness and significant achievement, the poet's last works which revolve around the idea of universal world theater.

The acts of this drama return at different planes of experience to the same central motifs. The end is a more complex and mature vision of the problems adumbrated in the earlier plays: first, the egoistical consciousness, the imprisoned ego, and the world about it; the transitoriness of things and the consequent necessity of human fidelity or devotion; then the missing and acquiring and achieving one's destiny;

and finally the mystery of action and suffering, guilt and sacrifice—in short, man's agony and glory "in coming to himself."

Thus, as Karl Naef has pointed out in *Hugo von Hof-mannsthals Wesen und Werk* (Zürich, 1938), the protagonists of Hofmannsthal's early playlets reappear sometimes as tragic heroes in later stages of development. For example, the fool Claudio, in *Death and the Fool*, caught short in his dreamlike, pre-existential mode of life, is the pagan forerunner of Everyman. And in general, the typical youthful figure of the short lyric dramas, hovering at the edge of life but suddenly awakened out of his dream to the realization of a wasted existence, a destiny missed, becomes at a later stage perhaps an Oedipus, boldly committed to life through guilt, the guiltless guilt of human action; or he may become, in a different idiom, the beggar of *The Great Theater of the World*, faced with a moral choice under the eyes of God and his angels upstage; or later still, he may go through all these phases to the point of transcending the arena of life, a Christ figure on earth, the prince Sigismund in *The Tower*.

The three plays selected here represent the major stages of Hofmannsthal's career in the modern theater, specifically his approach to the idea of a tragic theater. *Death and the Fool* (*Der Tor und der Tod*, 1893) is perhaps the best of the lyric dramas; certainly it is so as play, though some may prefer *The Little Theater of the World* (*Das Kleine Welttheater*, 1897) as poem. The dramatic conception of this one-act play, however simple theatrically it may appear to be, served Hofmannsthal as the groundwork of his later, more complex symbolistic stagecraft. *Electra* (1904) exemplifies his extensive experimentation with Greek themes during the first decade of the century: adaptations and original dramatizations, finished plays and synoptic drafts for unwritten tragedies. With the production of his new version of *Everyman*, Hofmannsthal discovered the possibilities of allegorical theater. *The Salzburg Great Theater of the World* (*Das Salzburger Grosse Welttheater*, 1922) illustrates the dramatic impact of transforming the theater so patently into the stage of life. Continuing in the same mode, though with important modifications, he wrote one of the masterpieces of contemporary drama, *The Tower* (*Der Turm*, 1925, 1927).

In the context of his total dramatic output, not to speak of his voluminous writings in other genres, this sequence reveals only one line of development, but it is crucial. It must be understood not merely as a development in dramatic technique, formally, but as a development of Hofmannsthal's *Lebensanschauung* which is reflected in all his writing. It would be a mistake, for example, to speak of these as his "serious" dramas to distinguish them from the comedies and the libretti, for his work, diverse as it may be in manner, is really of one piece.

Hofmannsthal himself pointed retrospectively to the web of speculative relations which joins his work in poetry, drama, and fiction from his earliest productions to the elaborate symbolist libretto, *The Woman Without a Shadow* (*Die Frau ohne Schatten*). Thus, the fool, Claudio, is shown to be related to several figures and themes in the lyric dramas and to motives touched on in the poems and stories. Ariadne and Zerbinetta in the operatic libretto, *Ariadne auf Naxos*, are a variation of the relationship between Electra and Chrysothemis.[7] And the subtle comedy of manners, *The Difficult Man* (*Der Schwierige*), barely hides the personal metaphysical element, the old problem, adumbrated in *Death and the Fool*, of the solitary individual bound to the society merely through language.[8] The list of connections could be extended beyond Hofmannsthal's own speculations on the unity of his poetic work. The poems, stories, comedies, and libretti are then equally serious, complementary expressions of his growing comprehension of man's estate in the world.

The poet's job is to fashion "the myth of the time." Hofmannsthal's sense of this mission was always with him. It accounts for his continuous struggle for subject, which was a struggle with himself and with his time, and his continuous experimentation with dramatic technique. Every work of art worthy of its name, he once wrote, includes the whole of human life. In the postwar years he devoted himself ardently to the task of forcing the stage to yield that totality. *The Great Theater of the World* and *The Tower* represent this effort in one direction; but late in life, apropos of *The Egyptian Helena*, he expressed his full-grown conviction that the mythological opera is the truest of art forms.[9]

II

The lyric one-acters, which Hofmannsthal wrote in his late teens and early twenties, make up only part of a rich production in that decade of poems, stories, essays, and reviews. On the basis of this youthful productivity between 1890 and 1899, he rose rapidly to fame. The piquancy of the situation was that under a pen name a schoolboy of sixteen had begun to turn out literature which many guessed at first to be the work of a seasoned, middle-aged artist. The literary world lionized the image of a young, inspired genius. But blind to Hofmannsthal's struggle to break out of the publicly created image of the pan-estheticist, it finally dropped the myth of the beautiful youth and along with it the maturing poet, when at the critical crossroad he broke forcibly away from the lyric and from what he manfully recognized as his years of literary apprenticeship. The poet in search of the road toward the ethically committed life and in search of a theater in which to represent the act of commitment ceased to interest his contemporaries, except for a few spiritual brothers who understood what he was about. An enchanted reading public had mistaken the intentions of a young man who, at the age of seventeen, could make the casual remark in a letter to a friend that the captain in the last act of *Lear* "betrays in five words the failure of a lifetime."

In his early lyric drama the young Hofmannsthal fashioned the image of the fin de siècle hero. He depicted his dramatic figures living, as it were, in a trance, imprisoned in palaces of pleasure and pain, and until the world makes its foreign demands upon them, the picture is itself entrancing. Understandably, the public often overlooked the ironic suggestions of hollowness. But the pre-existential hero, as Hofmannsthal called him, because of his childlike innocence of living experience—the burden of time is foreign to him—is no tragic hero. He is in his best moments ecstatically sensible of his mystical identity with every object about him, leading an exquisitely private and sensuous life, and yet he is always vaguely discontented, always anticipating the shock of recognizing that the world outside belongs in reality to itself. He senses that he inhabits a paradise of paralysis, and therefore he is afraid ironically of missing the reality of life.

In *Death and the Fool*, the most widely known of the lyric one-acters, Claudio strikes a near tragic note in his expression of remorse over the emptiness of his life, the tenuousness of his bond with the world, the lack of a personal destiny:

> Never on my way have I come upon the god
> With whom one strives until he grants his blessing.

These early playlets are no more than the prolog and epilog of a potential tragedy; they are like the monodies of prelapsarian Adams and Eves stuck into the world without being told so. The moment they become aware of their condition, the moment they see themselves ironically as in a mirror, they achieve tragic stature; but the spell is broken, the poem is done. Their comic counterpart in Hofmannsthal's theater is Casanova, the restless adventurer.

We know that the young poet himself went through this stage of uneasy suspension; in his best moments, moments of poetic creativity, he deemed himself precociously in possession of the world, but then again, he viewed longingly the world of men and action in the distance, beyond the walls of his garden. The antinomy between cognition and action must have become clear to him. He began to distrust the magic power of language; for "how can he who speaks still act," as he declares years later in a letter to his colleague, the dramatist Anton Wildgans, "since speech already implies cognition, and thus abrogates action."[10] He must have understood Hamlet's suspicion of language as an unreal bond between the solitary individual and society, the frivolity of his speech. Around the turn of the century, this problem developed into a personal crisis for Hofmannsthal.

He records it magnificently in the so-called "Letter of Lord Chandos" addressed to Francis Bacon.[11] In the guise of a Renaissance nobleman he describes his own critical experience at this time, the "estrangement from lyricism," as Hermann Broch calls it. For the poet who has lost the ecstatic sense of immanence, the world has become a foreign place, meaningless and incomprehensible, a conglomeration of dead *unnamable* objects. His alternatives are flight from the world, introversion, the way of mysticism, silence, or the attempt to apprehend and to express the phenomenal world in terms of action. For Hofmannsthal it was a personal as well as an artistic problem—to find the road which leads out of pre-existential isolation to the social and the active, to a life of commitment and participation.

Hence he broke deliberately with the mode of his early work in poetry and the lyric theater. The human soul must undergo the experience of time and yet remain devoted to its sense of timelessness. In a theater of tragic action he hoped to find the one instrument of expression whereby he could resolve the antinomy between speech and action, a problem which appeared to him to be of dramatic moment personally and also for his time. But by what sanctions does the tragic hero act? What are the sources of human destiny, what are the daemons inside the chosen, the tragic personality which impel him to do the deed which at once delivers and destroys? Preoccupied with such questions in the early years of the century, Hofmannsthal turned his attention to the great theaters of the past and experimented with a variety of tragic subjects in order to discover the ways of imitating the mystery of human action on the stage.

That the sanctions by which the dramatic hero acts should be the central problem for him is, of course, partly due to the personal crisis which he was undergoing; but it is also characteristic of the dilemma of the potential tragic poet in our time who must give the theater for which he writes a provisional social, philosophical, or religious orientation. Action on the Elizabethan stage, for example, is usually self-explanatory, its motives understood because it is usually referable to a conventional world view. The instructive exception for us here is *Hamlet*. It is the most problematical play in the Elizabethan repertory precisely because Shakespeare for once makes action itself problematical. Hamlet, the dispossessed prince, wants to find but cannot find in himself a satisfactory sanction for the deed. Therefore, he transforms every occasion for action into a melodrama of imagined action. The antinomy between cognition and action, between speaking and doing, remains also unresolved with him. And the dramatic tension derives from the necessity and his incapacity to assume the revenger's role, except "theatrically."

The double sense of the possibility and the necessity of commitment was for Hofmannsthal an enigma in tragedy which prevented him from easily imitating the mode either of Elizabethan drama or of the current realistic drama, both of which take independent action conventionally for granted. Nor, apparently, did the example of Calderón's theater offer at this time a satisfactory answer. *La Vida es Sueño* arrested his attention; Calderón's allegory exercised a fascination on him which lasted for the rest of his life. It ripened in his mind, and conversely he grew with its potentialities until he mastered it for his own purposes, a quarter of a century later, in his two versions of *The Tower*. For the moment, however, his attempt to make the subject his own resulted in a fragmentary experimental version.[12]

In his first experimentations with tragic drama (for example, his adaptation of Otway's *Venice Preserv'd* published in 1905), he tried to explore the road towards a timely tragedy by way of relating the ideas of human action and human destiny. The Catholic world view of Calderón subsumed this relationship without question. Calderón enacted allegorically the great drama of the Christian myth; Hofmannsthal was still in search of the myth of his time. He was looking for the daemons inside the tragic personality which compel it to do the necessary, self-sacrificial deed. The subjects of Greek mythology seemed to lend themselves more readily to his growing conception of a contemporary theater of tragic action.

Both Greek plays, *Electra* and *Oedipus and the Sphinx* (1906), turn upon the deed which is a self-willed necessity. It is unmotivated ethically, respondent only to a will which is, however, not merely shapeless impulse, but the will to become what one is, a tragic acceptance and fulfillment of the self. Electra embodies the doom on the house of Atreus. She and Clytemnestra are of one flesh, but Agamemnon's blood, which has been murderously shed, still courses through the girl's veins and demands revenge of the flesh.

> I know not how I should ever perish
> Except of this, that you should perish too.

This is spoken half ironically, but becomes literally true. Clytemnestra must die since Electra wills their common death, revenge and self-immolation in one.

All moral and social contingencies are stripped away from the situation. The question of right or wrong has no place in this portrait of a personality in the grip of a daemonic will power. Only the necessity of the deed and the superhuman effort to achieve it fills our imagination. The sacrifice of her girlhood, of her womanly shame, and her final self-sacrifice are no calculated course of action, nor yet an act of piety. She rejects Orestes' conventional remark that the gods have imposed this deed upon him. Her sacrifice is a self-willed necessity, and so should be a kind of blessed fulfillment.

For, as Hofmannsthal reminds us, she alone among the three women living in the ancestral home preserves the fidelity to what she is. She loses her individuality in order to save her self. He sees her as a young girl, sprung from the union of this father and this mother, turning not into a woman, but into a priestess without temple, without ritual, except the terrible ritual of blood. And she surrenders herself entirely to the primitive, severe law of fate which she herself embodies.[13] In the final scene, while Orestes kills the mother and her paramour inside the palace, Electra performs a "nameless" ecstatic dance of victory in the dusky courtyard and at this tense moment of her triumph she falls senseless to the ground. At that moment she symbolizes for Hofmannsthal simultaneously the sacrificing priest and the sacrificial animal, enacting the tragic ritual outside the palace walls. To do is to give one's self up.[14]

The youthful Oedipus in Hofmannsthal's *Oedipus and the Sphinx* is similarly capable of that total devotion of the self, of the momentary transition from pre-existential consciousness to unselfconsciousness, which the doing of a deed demands. There is a fascination in watching how each of his deeds makes actual the Delphic prophecy, how the young hero inevitably takes the road from Delphi to Thebes and finally stands at the cave of the Sphinx receiving his prize, the

hand of Jocasta. The homeless adventurer finds his way back
to the life of the community. The point is that Oedipus un-
derstands the Delphic oracle well; he knows what his race
is capable of:

> Wisely
> Respond the gods where we question foolishly.
> They despise the questions which we ask
> With our lips; but that which sleeps within
> Our inmost depths and has not waked to question
> Yet; to that their monstrous voice responds
> Beforehand.

In turning to Greek mythology for the subjects of his
drama Hofmannsthal sought to exemplify the interplay of
the free agent and necessity. Thus, Oedipus and Jocasta
actually master their mutually related fate, and half knowing,
half ignorant, they consecrate themselves freely to become
their own sacrificial victims. We should be lost in admira-
tion of this spectacle, were it not for our knowledge of their
piteous condition as they join hands and return in triumph to
Thebes. Their tragic dilemma is the universal human dilemma: they must act in virtual ignorance. Virtual ignorance,
not total ignorance. For Oedipus has dreamed the deep dream
of his life when the Delphic oracle designated him as the
sacrificial victim for the sins of his ancestral blood—to ex-
piate upon the father the passion to slaughter, and upon the
mother the lustful embrace. Oedipus and Jocasta, in Hofmannsthal's play, know and do not know that the dream of
Delphi is real, and that the sensual reality of the widowed
queen and the passionate youth is only delusion. Hence the
last scene sustains an almost unbearable tragic irony. Suspect-
ing a dangerous delusion and knowing the darkness, they still
surrender themselves, and so fulfill their destiny. They are at
once the chosen priests and the victims of the god.

"*Voluntas superior intellectu*"—thus Hofmannsthal describes the conception of a heroic personality who (quoting

Ibsen) "wills what he must because he is what he is and cannot act otherwise."[15] His distinctive personal character is itself the law of his actions, and his commitment, therefore, a total commitment. In tragedy such total commitment reunites the isolated sufferer with humanity, but at the cost of destruction and self-destruction. The tragic act is then to Hofmannsthal also a sacrificial act, in the sense that in every sacrificial act, the priest, or the actor, must at least for a moment be transformed into the victim and bleed and die and so give himself in order to validate the symbolic substitution.[16] So with Alcestis, Electra, and Oedipus.

This is provisionally the answer to the problem of tragic action which Hofmannsthal gives in terms of a modern theater dedicated to Dionysus, the invisible god inside the human animal. It is foreshadowed in a note which he had written as a young man, defining the fundamental tragic mythos in this way: The world dismembered into individuals longs for unity. Dionysus Zagreus wishes to be reborn. This is very much like Yeats's remark that "tragedy must always be a drowning and breaking of the dykes that separate man from man, and that it is upon these dykes comedy keeps house."

Though these two Greek dramas for the moment clarified for Hofmannsthal the problems of a theater of tragic action and successfully allegorized his sense of a personal and an epochal dilemma, namely the need to free the imprisoned self through a fatal act of commitment, yet they were bound to fail as the pattern of a modern idea of tragic theater. The material of the myths must naturally be divorced from its original context. In place of the religious orientation of the Athenian theater, Hofmannsthal created a modern Dionysiac theater; but though it was meant to do so, it failed to compel the contemporary audience to self-recognition with that immediacy which is indispensable in the theater.[17]

In a lecture in Oslo, in 1916, Hofmannsthal attempted to demonstrate a common idea behind his conception of the

Greek myth of Electra and of his Christian Everyman. In both, he said, the concept of individuality undergoes trial and question. Faced with ultimate demands, it dissolves. What does remain when the creature is totally stripped of the incidents of individuality? when all that is left is the lonely soul in need of deliverance? In both instances the answer lies in the word *fidelity* or devotion (*Treue*) to that which abides, to an absolute law, to the realm of Being. In a world in which everything is conceptualized in terms of becoming, or historicity, the poet must search for that which abides.

But what makes all the difference between Hofmannsthal's Greek theater and the Christian theater, as he develops it in the postwar years, is the definition of that realm of Being or the Law. In the one, deliverance comes to the tragic hero by way of fidelity to the self, to what he is; the Law, or the source of his destiny, lies in the hidden self, and the dream of Delphi discovers the gestures of the ancestral blood. In the other, deliverance comes by way of fidelity to the superpersonal, to the Christian order. The problem is to remember the forgotten law which death recalls: the Law is the Word. In both conceptions, the human act, motivated by such fidelity, causes suffering and delivers the patient. Actor and patient are one; priest and victim are one.

Hofmannsthal's Greek dramas create this tragic ritual and attempt to sanctify it, whereas the Christian festival plays imitate the prefigured religious ritual in allegorical terms, a celebration of the fall and the redemption. In the parlance of the drama we may call the one tragic action, the other, enactment. As the Christian drama focuses on the moment of conversion, spiritual rebirth, so the Dionysiac drama focuses on the moment of self-transformation, rebirth out of the self. But in the Christian conception blindness is no longer the unchangeable tragic condition of man; the Christian order, though invisible, is not inscrutable. Blindness is rather willful neglect of revealed Truth and therefore sin; it is tragic error, redeemable. Hence genuinely Christian drama is generally a form of divine comedy. It is pathetic when the creature commits the unforgivable sin and despairs. It is tragic, in human eyes, when the protagonist necessarily re-enacts the fall and gains deliverance only in the midst of destruction. It is great tragic drama when the playwright, instead of merely availing himself of the conventional belief in a universal order, each time recreates that order; for it must be achieved dramatically, not pointed to referentially. The protagonist must *become* a Christian hero; his *knowledge* of the way should be irrelevant. Hofmannsthal had a keener artistic sense of this problem than Eliot did when, in the followng decade, he dramatized the martyrdom of Thomas à Becket.

III

It was the Christian dramatic idiom by which Hofmannsthal finally achieved the goal of a meaningful contemporary theater. His version of *Everyman* had been an early start in this direction, and its production in Salzburg confirmed the appeal and the timely significance of such a theater. The idea of allegorical world theater explains itself in Hofmannsthal's modern mystery play, *The Salzburg Great Theater of the World*, which was produced in 1922. Again a multiple stage structure was erected, this time, by special permission of the archbishop, inside one of Salzburg's impressive baroque churches. Here the scaffold does not merely serve as a magic mirror for the visible world and its invisible order, as in *Everyman*, but the idea of man as a player on the world's stage becomes the very principle of the mise en scène. For God, the master, speaking from the top of the scaffold, actually orders the world to produce a play under his eyes, featuring man who is to act out his part on earth.

Six unborn souls are brought forward to be invested with their individual roles in life. Created free and in the image of God, each must face his destiny. It is an improvised play, the plot undetermined. Only its title is given: Act righteously! God is above you! But before the production gets under way, the World, as stage manager, has a bit of trouble assembling her cast. Five of the actors accept their parts willingly and submit to their incarnation as king, rich man, farmer, Beauty, and Wisdom; only the soul destined to be the beggar, having looked over his difficult role, refuses to take part in the drama of life. He throws aside the patched rags which are to be his costume and tries, though in vain, to tear his parchment scroll into shreds.

At once the Adversary, dressed in the habit of a scholarly logician, stands at the rebel's side and makes a formally legal demand for the natural equality of destinies. Why should of two guiltless souls one be created Jacob and another Esau? The question in behalf of the rebellious soul is crucial, though we understand that the devil should know better than to ask it so ingenuously. An angel must intervene, speaking from the upper stage, and he succeeds at last in instructing the rebellious soul in the mystery of human freedom: What the actor *does* gives meaning to his part. The free human choice, the deed alone, creates above creation itself. For though there are these words in the beggar's part: my God, why hast Thou forsaken me?—there is also this line: not my will, but Thine be done. And so the soul accepts his costume and his role with resolution.

But as soon as the play gets under way on the lower level of the stage structure, all the actors except Wisdom forget the theatrical condition of their existence; they are caught up so completely in their earthly roles. For the spectator, however, the two worlds of passing time and eternity or of playacting and reality are always spatially juxtaposed. Hofmannsthal suggests the significant connection between them in terms of the human act, the transcendent deed, which delivers the actor. The beggar's difficult and miserable role in the world has brought him understandably to the point of desperation and rebellious rage. His murderous axe swings high over his head, an instrument with which to demolish the visible order of injustice. But it is the dramatic moment of a misdeed averted, the moment of conversion, by which the beggar transcends the mundane order of creation.

By an act of grace—Saul responding to the blinding sheet of light from heaven—the beggar suddenly sees the *whole* stage of life relumined. In terms of the world's play, his part has been the least; but in God's eyes it is Jacob's part. And as the passage of time, translated into a rhythmic dance of death, destroys beauty, wealth, and power, the hierarchy is reversed. For when Death calls the actors one by one to leave the world's stage and to resign their costumes, it is the beggar who leads the disembodied souls up before the palace of the master while the rich man kneels below. The *De Profundis* sounds in the distance.

Though Hofmannsthal has sharply focused his drama on the topical problem, in the postwar years, of social and economic inequality and on the corruption of traditional authority, he has yet retained the character of the mystery of Calderón's Corpus Christi play, *El Gran Teatro del Mundo*, on which *The Great Theater of the World* is based. The king who has himself corrupted God's order on earth strides but for a brief moment across the world's stage; he is always a player king. But it is the beggar who recollects that he is playing in a borrowed costume which must soon be returned; he remembers the mise en scène of life. Therefore, he drops the axe and withdraws into the stillness of the forest, choosing the Franciscan contemplative life until Death recalls him to appear before the king of kings, before God the Father, in whose sight all children are equal and free.[18]

The beggar's decision amounts to a denial of the reality

of any time-bound order which distorts the image of the eternal order. In refusing, by his sudden illumination, to destroy the world's false authority, he has done the deed which creates above creation itself. He has that rare spiritual gift, which we noted in Oedipus in a different context, of being born anew. But here it is the Pauline mystery which redeems his blindness and transforms the potentially tragic temporal moment into divine comedy. With this play Hofmannsthal sets the stage for his last tragedy, *The Tower*.

In *The Great Theater of the World* the ironic condition of playacting is always held before our eyes. The double perspective on man's action on the world's stage affords us a kind of reassurance, for the cosmic setting of the mystery play allows us to judge the doings of man in time by the eternal order of God and his angelic spokesmen; the converted beggar can simply withdraw from the scene of human folly and injustice and outlast the bonds of time. By the grace of God, the beggar escapes guilt. But for prince Sigismund in *The Tower*, betrayed by the king, his father, guilt is a condition of life.[19] He becomes, therefore, tragic actor and sacrificial victim in one. In this last play, Hofmannsthal still retains the allegorical approach, but one half of the theatrical metaphor "The world is God's stage" has disappeared. The top level of the scaffold is gone, and the actors play their tragic roles in a fabulous historic setting. Only the protagonist remembers in the end the condition of his existence.

The Tower is based on the old story, which goes back beyond Calderón's *La Vida es Sueño*, of the prince imprisoned in a tower from the time of his birth because his royal father fears a prophecy of insurrection and the loss of his throne. Though Hofmannsthal uses this ancient motif and retains some of the figures of Calderón's drama, he radically reshaped the play in the course of many years during which he pondered the subject. The metaphor of life as a dream does not chiefly inform the new play; he rather builds upon it his own tragic structure. The experience of the first world war and its aftermath in central Europe, the vision of a world in dissolution, a tradition demolished, at last rendered the full possibilities of the subject conceivable.

As the material of *The Tower* takes shape in his mind, Hofmannsthal sees it as the tragedy of a time-bound world gone astray, a world which needs deliverance in the person of a savior; for it is altogether deprived of the sound of God's voice and suffers the torments of guilt. But the potential savior of a forsaken humanity is himself human. Drawn into a world which is torn by rebellion and suppression, he suffers the tragic fate of all humanity betrayed in the life-and-death struggle of contending powers. In the figure of Sigismund, Hofmannsthal represents first the allegory of the Fall, man's tragic attempt to capture the world into which he is thrust, and the individual's tragic subjection to time, conceived as history.

Betrayed from the moment of his birth, the prince lingers in his tower, suffering the bodily torment of imprisonment in a cage as well as the spiritual torment of imprisonment inside the self; he does not know where the "I" ends and where the world begins. The physician alone recognizes both the betrayal of humanity at large by this uncompleted murder of a human life and the untouchable dignity of the creature before him. He alone sees the connection between the foundering of a whole kingdom and the disfiguration of a human life. The governor of the tower, Count Julian, sets the dramatic action in motion by persuading the king to receive his unacknowledged son. A political opportunist, Julian stakes his life on the success of the trial. But when the prince is born again, as it were, out of the tower of suffering into a world of corrupted authority and anarchy, and must undergo the supreme test of facing his father, he responds naturally with passionate human indignation; his first act in this dark world incurs the guilt of rebellion. For though Sigismund has been taught the meaning of creator and creature, he finds instead of a father the corrupted image of a king.

His humanly frail response to force with force inevitably fails. The task which a desperate time demands of him is other than that. His part is not possessing the world; he must found it anew. It imposes the role of savior on a time-bound creature. For he represents a cause larger than his individual redemption from guilt; his name and figure have stirred messianic hopes in the hearts of the poor and the oppressed. He is the nameless beggar king who comes in chains to deliver them. His personal fate is now identical with the historic fate of the kingdom. And so he stands alone surrounded by the warring factions which his rebellion has set loose: a maddened absolute power, the ruling king; an idealist revolutionary power, the ambitious Count Julian; a proud and loveless ecclesiastic power, the retired cardinal, Brother Ignatius; and a newly unshackled ruthless power, the iron-clad figure of Olivier, the leader of a lawless mob. The grim play of these uncontrollable factions centered on Sigismund's person symbolizes a gigantic psychomachy for the salvation of humanity.

So far, the story of the prince recalls Hofmannsthal's preoccupation since his earliest work with the potentially tragic conditions of man's existence in the world. Sigismund is the last of an array of dramatic figures who in action and in suffering, boldly and timidly, attempt to discover the road leading out of the tower of the solitary self into the dangerous world. In this, the largest of his dramas, Hofmannsthal poses once more the basic problem of all his work. In his notebooks he returns in several places to the same statement of it: Two antinomies are to be resolved, that of passing time and permanence, and that of solitude and community. Without faith in eternity no true life is possible. This line in *Death and the Fool*, he concludes, was decisive: "I shall learn fidelity which is the mainstay of all life."[20]

Sigismund's tragedy is then the tragedy of being born

human, an impotent creature of clay, killing vermin in his animal cage, and yet born in the image of God, inviolable and spiritually strong enough to bear the world's burden on his shoulders, if he could find his way into the world. But there is also the tragedy of a world in the grip of revolution which receives him Judas-like. He is tested by the king and, later, he is tested by the mob; neither power finds him useful, and neither power recognizes his identity.

According to the testimony of a close friend, Hofmannsthal apparently suffered in the extended course of his composition from a more than usually deep and personal involvement in this tragic testing of human durability. In the early twenties, his letters speak of his work on *The Tower* as "an almost mysterious labor." Plainly stated, the artistic problem was

> to render distinctly the breaking-in of chaotic forces in a worldly order which rests no longer on spiritual foundations; against the dark background the victim must stand out plastically, the imprisoned prince, who alone undertakes the struggle in himself with the help of that spiritual strength which he has acquired through suffering.[21]

But if the allegory of the initial acts defined his tragic vision truthfully, then the conclusion could offer nothing but a catastrophe of the grimmest order, unthinkable hopelessness, chaos come again. For years Hofmannsthal struggled with himself to avoid that admission of absolute defeat in the face of absolute power. He had shuddered over the dark conclusions in Shakespeare. If deliverance is impossible to find in the human scene, then it must lie beyond, he thought, in the realm of those living powers which sustain the world above nothingness. And in the first version of 1925, the book version of the play, after a long and desperate struggle over the last act, he finally managed to wrest a conclusion from the material.[22]

Here, following the rebellion against his father, Sigismund has been returned to the tower, which is now his castle and his grave. Locked inside himself, himself an impregnable fortress, he chooses to stand firm in his prison. The phenomenal world of power and passion outside his fortress is to him indeed a world of dreams, unreal. But the forces of revolt break into Sigismund's sufficient kingdom and bring with them the pungent smell of fire and blood. And he hears above the violence confronting him the cry of a wretched humanity. The tragic act of sacrifice and self-sacrifice is demanded of him. Clutching a jug of water to slake his thirst, he steps slowly once more into the burning world outside.

The language of the battlefield issues in strange accents from his mouth; he has had to learn it from inward strength and necessity. He reads Plutarch and Aurelius to learn his new and difficult role. Julian's disciple of the tower has been drawn into this world, but he is not of this world. Hence the climactic scene in the last act where he battles with demons instead of armies. Olivier's diabolic forces are defeated in this earlier version of the play, yet in the symbolic battle of spirits in which Sigismund engages alone in his general's tent he emerges victor only at the cost of his own life. Though he has cleansed the world by his personal sacrifice, his strength is only the strength of the impregnable tower of which he is still king and master. It is not for him to create a new order out of the shambles of the old; he is the saintly interim king, the sacrificed liberator and deliverer, who may only glimpse the promised land. His grave will consecrate the land.

Hofmannsthal's conclusion to this version of the play raises a historically conceived situation into the realm of myth. He confesses that it has something about it of a castle built over a bottomless void. The dying Sigismund leaves the racked kingdom in the hands of a mythical boy-king leading an army of orphan children, the victims and the only hope of a bloody time, who can restore the world to the ways of peace and brotherly love. Incredible as this solution may seem following the terrors of the play up to that point, it is yet a powerful symbolic gesture of faith, born out of a sense of despair. For Hofmannsthal it is a poetic adjuration of those invisible powers which, he felt, could alone sustain the world above the void. In the context of the play, this is not an instance of deus ex machina, but rather a return to the religious and dramatic conception of the world as a stage. The mythological ending has the conviction of Aeschylus' conclusion to the *Oresteia* trilogy.

Two years later, in 1927, Hofmannsthal finished the present version of *The Tower*. Encouraged by Max Reinhardt to change the last two acts, to shorten the tragedy and render it playable, Hofmannsthal undertook a thorough revision for the theater. But he must first have yielded to a more radical voice of persuasion coming from himself. The play before us answers to a new mandate of poetic justice; it is an unflinching, historic testimony and a moving personal confession that the gathering night cannot be shut out. A more austere dramatic economy informs the revised version, and the action moves relentlessly to its stark conclusion. Here the coup d'état, engineered by Julian, succeeds. The old king, Sigismund's father, is forced to abdicate. Yet Sigismund is now more conspicuously the sacrificial victim. He has the strength to preserve his integrity; but he moves like a disembodied spirit through the turmoil of clashing factions. The nobles, then Julian, and finally Olivier try to use this meek figure on the throne to further their own ends. They need his counterfeit, but Sigismund himself remains untouchable and therefore unusable. Like the converted beggar of *The Great Theater of the World*, his eyes have been opened; he is ripe. But in the tragic world of *The Tower* the prince cannot withdraw; and when Olivier stands at last before him, covered cap-à-pie with leather and iron, the war club in his hand *is* the ultimate power in this world. Though Sigismund's spirit remains unimpaired—"I feel far too well to hope"—yet he recognizes his tragic failure to find his way out of the tower, which is still his prison and the source of his strength: "Bear witness, I was here, though no one has known me."

Since its publication, *The Tower* appears to have become the poetic chronicle of our time. It is that rare instance in our time of a tragedy which touches at so many points the human situation essentially and the politics of human action historically that it belongs with the best traditional examples of great theater. The lifelong search after dramatic subject and form in which to express fully his sense of the time led Hofmannsthal to experiment with a number of dramatic modes. But it was in the idea of allegorical world theater, the mode of *Everyman* and Calderón, that he discovered the most comprehensive form of playing.

A conviction similar to Eliot's that "the theater has reached a point at which a revolution in principles should take place" ("Four Elizabethan Dramatists," 1924) must have prompted Hofmannsthal from the beginning to avoid the contemporary theater of realism which offered its own ready conventions, however restrictive, and to return to the tradition of representing the mysteries of the theater of real life allegorically on a popular stage. He assumed in his dramatic work a point of view transcending the business being transacted on the stage; his characters represent not real men in action, but players in symbolic situations drawn from the theater of real life. In the two festival plays Hofmannsthal realized this conception of the world as the great stage on which mankind plays the drama of life. The same conception, though not ostensible in the setting, informs the tragic action of *The Tower*. In this way, Hofmannsthal succeeded in recreating an ample and representative theater in which to mirror the tragedy of a century of totalitarian ways of life.

Notes

1. See "Deutsche Festspiele zu Salzburg" (1919), and "Festspiele in Salzburg" (1919), *Prosa III* (Frankfurt a. M., 1952) in *Gesammelte Werke*, ed. Herbert Steiner. Hofmannsthal's essays on the festival theater are conveniently collected in *Festspiele in Salzburg* (Frankfurt a. M., 1952).

2. "Festspiele in Salzburg," *Prosa III*, pp. 448-49.

3. "Aufzeichnungen zu Reden in Skandinavien," *Prosa III*, p. 353.

4. Trans. by Vernon Watkins in *Selected Plays and Libretti*, Bollingen Series 33, III (New York, 1963). Cf. E. R. Curtius, "George, Hofmannsthal und Calderón" (1934), *Kritische Essays zur europäischen Literatur* (Bern, 1950), on the significance of Hofmannsthal's orientation toward the "timeless Middle Ages" and Calderón's theater.

5. *Selected Prose*, Bollingen Series 33, I (New York, 1952), 350.

6. "Das alte Spiel von Jedermann" (1912), *Prosa III*, pp. 115-16.

7. See the unique set of philosophical and critical notes on his own work, entitled *Ad me ipsum*, first published by Walther Brecht, now more easily accessible in *Die Neue Rundschau*, LXV (1954), 358 ff. (and in *Aufzeichnungen* [Frankfurt a. M., 1959], *Gesammelte Werke*).

8. Joseph A. von Bradish, "Der Briefwechsel Hofmannsthal-Wildgans," *PMLA*, XLIX (1934), 947.

9. "Die ägyptische Helena," *Prosa IV* (1955), p. 460.

10. Bradish, p. 947.

11. Trans. by Tania and James Stern in *Selected Prose*, pp. 129-41.

12. On the successive stages of Hofmannsthal's play and their relation to his other work, see Grete Schaeder, "Hugo von Hofmannsthals Weg zur Tragödie (Die drei Stufen der Turm-Dichtung)," *Deutsche Vierteljahrsschrift für Literaturwissenschaft und Geistesgeschichte*, XXIII (1949), 306-50. In the ensuing discussion I follow the lead of this essay in emphasizing Hofmannsthal's concern with the problem of action and the enigma of the tragic act, both in his critical notes and in the plays themselves.

13. "Aufzeichnungen zu Reden in Skandinavien," pp. 354-55.

14. *Ad me ipsum*, pp. 361, 364. Electra is essentially passive at the point of crisis; Orestes does the deed. Yet she dies of the accomplished deed. Her relation to the deed is treated ironically, Hofmannsthal says, and he appends the suggestive notation: Electra-Hamlet.

15. "Aufzeichnungen zu Reden in Skandinavien," p. 351.

16. See the discussion of this symbolic act in "Das Gespräch über Gedichte," *Prosa II* (1951), pp. 103-4; cited by Schaeder, p. 323 (and first elaborated in her earlier study, *Die Gestalten* [Berlin, 1933], pp. 75-77, 82-83).

17. The perennial success of *Electra* as an opera is due to the fact that Hofmannsthal's text is also an admirable libretto. Richard Strauss's music provides that theatrical immediacy by reinterpreting the tragedy in strictly sensuous terms.

18. Cf. Schaeder, pp. 331-32.

19. *Ibid.*, p. 334.

20. *Ad me ipsum*, pp. 361, 367, 369.

21. Carl J. Burckhardt, *Erinnerungen an Hofmannsthal und Briefe des Dichters* (Basel, 1944), pp. 36, 40, 56, 67-68.

22. Trans. by Michael Hamburger in *Selected Plays and Libretti*.

Death and the Fool

Characters

DEATH
CLAUDIO, A NOBLEMAN
HIS VALET
CLAUDIO'S MOTHER ⎫
A MISTRESS OF CLAUDIO ⎬ *Dead persons*
A FRIEND OF HIS YOUTH ⎭

(Claudio's house. Costumes of the twenties of the last century.)

(Claudio's study, in Empire style. In the background, left and right, large windows; in the center a glass door opening out on the balcony from which a suspended wooden staircase leads down into the garden. On the left, a white folding door, on the right, a similar one into the bedroom, closed off by a green velvet curtain. Near the window, left, a writing desk in front of which stands an armchair. Against the doorposts, glass cases with antiques. On the wall, right, a gothic chest carved in dark wood; above it antique musical instruments. An almost blackened painting by an Italian master. The ground color of the wallpaper is light, almost white, with stuccowork and gold.)

CLAUDIO *(alone)*

(He sits by the window. Light of the setting sun.)

Now the farthest mountains lie glowing in the light,
Draped in the moistened glaze of sun-drenched air.
A crown of alabaster clouds is drifting
High above, gray shadows, framed in gold:
Thus did the masters of bygone days

Paint clouds which uplift the Madonna.
Blue cloud-shadows lie across the slopes,
The mountain-shadow fills the open valley
And dims the lustrous meadows to a grayish green;
The last full beam kindles the mountain peak.
How near to my heart's desire have they come
Who dwell in solitude on those far slopes,
Whose goods and chattels, reaped with their hands,
Reward the pleasant weariness of limbs.
The wonderful wild morning wind, who runs
Barefoot through the sweetness of the heath,
He awakens them; the wild bees are
Around them and God's bright burning air.
In nature they have found their daily tasks,
And nature is the spring of all their desires;
Their strength by turns refreshed and spent,
They feel the touch of each warm happiness.
Now sinks the golden globe and disappears
In the crystal green of far-off seas;
The last light glistens through distant trees,
Now red vapor breathes, a sheet of fire
Inundates the shore, where the cities lie
Which with naiad-arms, thrust from the flood,
Gently rock their children in tall ships,
A people, bold, cunning, and illustrious.
They glide through faraway, wondrous slow
And silent waves which no keel has ever cleft.
The wrath of savage seas stirs the breast
And cures it so of every folly and pain.
Thus I see purpose and blessing spread before me
And filled with longing I gaze forever across,
But as I turn my eyes on nearer things,
All becomes empty, more grievous and drear;
It seems that my whole life thus let slip by,
Lost joys and unwept tears, moves and twists

About these streets, this house, and endless
Senseless searching, troubled longing.

(*Standing near the window*)

Now they are lighting their lamps and they have
Within their narrow walls a dim world
With all the gifts of revelry and tears
And whatever else can captivate a heart.
Their hearts are close to one another
And they grieve for someone far away;
And if perchance one came to harm
They comfort him . . . I have never learned to comfort.
They know how to say with simple words
What is needed for tears and for laughter.
They need not pound with bleeding fists
Against the seven nailed-up gates.

What should I know of human life?
To be sure, I stood in the midst of it,
But at best I have comprehended it,
Could never get enmeshed in it,
Have never lost my self to it.
Where others take, where others give
I have stood apart, a dumb-born heart.
Never have I on all these loving lips
Tasted the true draught of life;
Never, shaken by true sorrow, never!
Have I walked, lonely and sobbing, along my way.
If ever I did feel one breath,
One touch of nature's goodly gifts,
My ever restless reason, unable to forget,
Would call it by its glaring name.
And then as a thousand resemblances rushed
To the mind, all trust, all happiness was gone.
And even sorrow! Frayed and worn

To shreds by thinking, faded and blanched!
Oh, how I wished to press it to my breast,
What joy I would have drawn out of the pain:
It brushed me with its wing, and I grew faint,
Discomfort came in place of pain. . .

(Starting up)

It is growing dark. I begin to brood.
Well, well: time has children of all kinds.
But I am tired and ought to sleep.

(The valet brings a lamp, and goes again.)

Now by lamplight I can see again
This lumber-room littered with dead things,
By which, although I never found
The direct way, I thought I stole
Into that life for which I yearned.

(In front of the crucifix)

Some have lain at your wounded feet of ivory,
O Lord upon the cross, praying for the flames,
Those sweet flames which wondrously inspirit,
To descend into their hearts; and when
Barren coldness came instead of glowing flame,
They perished with fear, remorse, and shame.

(In front of an old painting)

You, Gioconda, gleaming from a marvelous
Surface with the glow of animate limbs,
The mysterious mouth, both harsh and sweet,
With the splendor of eyelids heavy with dreams;
You betrayed to me just so much of life
As I could, questioning, breathe into you!

(*Turning away, in front of a chest*)

You, goblets, how many lips have fondly
Touched your cooling rim; and you,
Ancient lutes, whose strain has unsealed
In many a heart its deepest emotion,
What would I give, could you enchant me too;
Oh, that I were captive to your spell!
You, counterfeits in wood and bronze,
Carved forms, bewildering rush of shapes,
You toads, angels, griffins, fauns,
Fantastic birds, golden garlands of fruit,
Intoxicating, terrifying things,
Once you must have all been felt,
Engendered by living quivering fancies,
Washed ashore out of the great sea
And caught in the form like the fish in the net!
In vain, I have pursued you, all in vain,
Too much taken with your charm:
And as I let each of your self-willed souls,
Like your masks, possess my inmost feelings,
There dropped a veil over life and heart and world;
You held me surrounded, a fluttering horde,
Devouring, inexorable harpies,
Each fresh flowering near fresh springs. . .
I had so lost myself to artificial things
That I saw the sun with lifeless eyes
And heard no longer but with lifeless ears:
And always I dragged this mysterious curse,
Never quite aware, never wholly unaware,
With small sorrow and stale delight
To live my life like a book, half of which
One cannot yet and half one does no longer understand,
And only afterwards the mind seeks out the breath of life—

And that which gave me pain and gave me pleasure,
I felt as if it never meant itself,
No, but borrowed glimpse of future time
And hollow image of a fuller life.
And thus in sorrow and in every joy
Bewildered I fought only with shadows,
Used up, but not enjoyed my every impulse,
In a torpid dream that at last the day would break.
I turned and looked upon this life:
Where being swift is of no use, running,
And being brave does not help in strife,
Where misfortune makes not sad and happiness not glad;
Senseless questions come to senseless answers;
A tangled dream arises from the darkened cave,
And chance is all, time, wind, and wave!
Thus, sorrowful and wise, cherishing disillusioned
Thoughts in weary pride, deeply sunk
In resignation, thus without complaint
I go on living in these rooms, in this town.
The people here no longer question me;
They find that I am rather commonplace.

> (*The valet comes and sets a plate full of cherries
> on the table; he is about to close the balcony door.*)

CLAUDIO

Do not yet shut the doors . . . What frightens you?

VALET

Your Lordship won't believe me.

> (*Half to himself, frightened*)

Now they have hidden in the summerhouse.

CLAUDIO

Who has?

VALET

Begging your pardon, but I don't know.
A whole crowd of the most fearsome rabble.

CLAUDIO

Beggars?

VALET

I do not know.

CLAUDIO

Then lock the door,
The garden door into the street,
And go to bed and let me be.

VALET

That's just what frightens me. I have already
Locked the garden door. But now . . .

CLAUDIO

Well?

VALET

Now they're sitting in the garden; on the bench
Where the sandstone Apollo stands. A few of them
In the shade over there by the edge of the fountain,
And one sits on top of the Sphinx.
You cannot see him; the yew tree covers him.

CLAUDIO

Are they men?

VALET

Some of them, yes. But women too.
Not beggarly, only old-fashioned in their dress,

In the manner of old engravings. But to sit there
In that fearful way, perfectly still
And looking with lifeless eyes at you
As if gazing into empty space. No!
They are not of human kind. If it please
Your Honor, be not vexed with me, but I would not
Go near them, not for all the world.
God willing, they'll be gone tomorrow morning;
By your gracious leave, my Lord, I will now
Bolt and lock the door of the house
And sprinkle holy water on the lock.
Because I have never seen such men before,
And human kind doesn't have such eyes.

CLAUDIO

Do as you please, and good night.

> (*He walks up and down for a while, lost in thought.
> Offstage the sound of a violin playing a melody touched
> with longing and emotion, at first from a distance, gradu-
> ally nearer, and at last, warm and rich, as if it came from
> the adjoining room.*)

                              Music?
And strangely speaking to the soul!
Has that fellow's madness touched me too?
It seems as if I had never heard
Such strains played by human hands...

> (*He stands still, turned towards the right side, listening.*)

Like a deep and seemingly long-wished-for
Thrill it runs through me irresistibly;
It seems to be an infinite regret,
Infinite hopefulness it seems to be,
As if out of these old, silent walls

My life came streaming and translucent down on me.
Like my beloved one's or like my mother's coming,
Like every long-lost-one's return,
It stirs up thoughts of warmth and devotion
And flings me into a sea of youth:
A boy, I stood thus in vernal splendor
And fancied I soared up into the universe;
An immense longing beyond all bounds
Surged through me like a portentous flood!
And there came the time to travel, a time of ecstasy,
When now and again the whole world shone,
And roses glowed, and bells rang out,
Exulting and illumined with a strange light:
How full of life all things were then,
Within close reach of loving apprehension,
How I felt myself inspired and enrapt,
A living link in the great circle of life!
Then I divined, still guided by my heart,
The stream of Love which nourishes all hearts
And an abundance swelled my being which
Today yet scarcely exalts my dream.
Keep on, music, a short while longer thus,
And stir deep down my inmost self:
I could easily deem my life to be warm and gay
If thus bewitched I may relive its course:
For all sweet flames, licking tongues of fire,
Shoot up now, melting all rigidity!
Seized by this sound of primal conscience,
By these childish-deep strains, the heavy burden
Of knowledge, far too old and too confused,
Heaped upon these shoulders, lifts.
From afar with a mighty ringing of bells
A scarcely imagined life proclaims itself,
In forms which are infinitely meaningful,
Prodigious-yet-plain both in giving and taking.

(*The music stops almost abruptly.*)

There, sudden silence! What has moved me so deeply,
Wherein I have felt the god in man, has grown dumb!
And he who unwittingly sent up this magic world,
Most likely he holds out his cap, begging for a coin,
A wandering musician on his nightly round.

(*Near the window, right*)

He does not stand down here. How strange!
Where else? I will look through the other window. . .

(*As he walks to the door on the right, the curtain is
gently pulled back, and inside the door stands Death, the
fiddle-bow in his hand, the violin hanging from his belt.
He looks quietly at Claudio who recoils terror-stricken.*)

What senseless nameless fear lays hold of me!
If the sound of your fiddle was so lovely,
Then why this fit of pain to look at you?
What constricts my throat and stiffens the hair?
Begone! You are Death himself. What would you here?
I am afraid. Begone! I cannot cry.

(*Sinking*)

My strength, the very breath of life is leaving me!
Go! Who called you? Go! Who let you in?

DEATH

Get up! Throw off this inherited fear!
I am not frightful, I am no skeleton!
Kinsman to Dionysus and to Venus,
A great god of the soul stands before you.
When in the mild mid-summer's eve
A leaf drifted down through the golden air,
My fluttering breath caused you to shudder,
Which hovers dreamlike around ripe things.

When the surging swell of feelings filled
The trembling soul with a warm flood,
When in a sudden thrilling flash, the awesome,
The unearthly revealed itself as kindred,
And you, surrendering your self
To the great round dance, took the world as your own:
In every truly supreme hour
Which caused your earthly form to shudder,
I touched the springs of your soul
With a holy, mysterious power.

CLAUDIO

Enough. I greet you, though my heart is uneasy.

(Short pause)

But for what real purpose did you come?

DEATH

My coming, friend, has always but *one* meaning!

CLAUDIO

With me there is yet time for *that!*
Remember: before the leaf glides to the ground
It has drained all the sap and is done!
I am far short of that: I have not lived!

DEATH

But you have gone your way like everyone!

CLAUDIO

As flowers uprooted in the fields
Are swept downstream by black water,
So my young days have slipped away,
And I never knew that even this meant life.
Then . . . I stood before the trellised gates of life,

Trembling before its wonders, stung with sweet longing,
That with majestic peals of thunder they should
Fly asunder, miraculously shattered.
It did not happen so . . . and then I stood inside,
Devoid of grace, and could not recollect
My own self and all my deepest desires,
Overpowered by a curse which did not end.
Bewildered by twilight and as if entombed,
Peevish and deeply troubled inwardly,
Halfhearted, my senses paralyzed,
In every consummation mysteriously curbed,
I never felt my inner self enveloped with fire,
Nor ever really swept by mighty waves;
Never on my way have I come upon the god
With whom one strives until he grants his blessing.

DEATH

What was given to all was also given to you,
A mortal life to live upon this earth.
A spirit wells up stanchly inside all of you
Which bids you animate this chaos
Of dead things with relatedness
And make your garden out of it
For usefulness, contentment and distress,
Woe to you if I must tell you this!
One binds and one is bound in turn,
Thriving in the wild and sultry hours,
Cried to sleep and worn with toil,
Still desiring, heavy with longing, half despairing,
Breathing deeply and warm with the pulse of life. . .
Yet all, once *ripe*, must fall into my arm.

CLAUDIO

But I am not ripe, so leave me here.
I will no longer foolishly lament,

I shall cling to this clod of earth,
The deepest longing for life cries out in me.
The utmost fear is breaking the ancient curse;
Now I feel—oh, let me—that I can live!
I feel it by this boundless thrust;
I can fasten my heart to earthly things.
Oh, you shall see, no longer like dumb beasts
Or playthings will others be to me!
They and all that is theirs shall speak to my heart;
I shall force my way to every joy and pain.
I will learn fidelity, which is the mainstay
Of all life . . . I will so yield myself
That good and evil shall have power
Over me and make me free and glad.
Then will these shadows come to life for me!
Men I shall find along my way,
No longer dumb in taking and giving;
To be bound by others—yes!—and strongly bind.

(*As he notices Death's unmoved expression, he continues
with increasing fear.*)

Look now, believe me, it has not been so till now:
You think I must have loved and hated . . .
No, never did I grasp its real sense,
An exchange it was of words and pretence, empty!
Here, look, I can show you: Letters, do you see,

(*He flings open a drawer and takes from it bundles of
neatly arranged old letters.*)

Full of oaths and words of love and lament;
Do you think I ever *felt* what *they*—
Or *felt* what *I* seemed to say in reply?!

(*He throws the bundles at Death's feet so that single
letters fall out.*)

Here you have this love life, all of it,
Which re-echoes my own self and only myself
As I, throbbing with the ups and downs
Of my instant mood, scorned every sacred tie!
There, there! and everything else like this:
Without sense, without joy, without pain, without love,
    without hate!

DEATH

You fool! You wretched fool, I will teach you
Once to honor life before you leave it.
Stand there, be silent and look here
And learn that all others sprang from this sod
With a deep-rooted love of the earth.
And you alone, a hollow and vain fool.

> (*Death plays a few notes on his violin as though calling
> someone. He stands near the bedroom door, in the fore-
> ground on the right; Claudio, by the wall, left, in semi-
> darkness. Out of the door, right, comes the mother. She
> is not very old. She wears a long black velvet gown, a
> black velvet cap with a white frill which frames her face.
> In her delicate pale fingers a white lace handkerchief.
> She steps softly through the door and walks silently
> about the room.*)

THE MOTHER

How many sweet pains I inhale
With this air. Like a gentle dead breeze
Of lavender half of my earthly
Existence blows about this room:
Yes, a mother's life, one part pain,
Part toil, and part care. What could a man
know of this?

(*Near the chest*)

This edge here, still sharp?
He fell here once and cut his forehead;
Of course, he was a small and fiery child,
Running wildly, impossible to hold.
There, the window! I stood here often and strained
Into the night, listening with such eagerness
For the sound of his step, when fear would not let me sleep,
When he did not come and the clock struck two, and then
Struck three and the pale day began to break. . .
How often . . . Yet he never knew—
And by day I was also much alone.
The hand, it waters the flowers, pounds dust
From the cushion, shines the brass latch on the door,
And so the day passes; but the head,
It has nothing to do: a dreary wheel
Goes round in a circle, with forebodings
And a mysterious nightmarish feeling of pain,
Which must be bound up with the secret,
Incomprehensible sanctity of motherhood
And with all the deepest living motions
Of this world. But I may no longer
Breathe of the sweetly oppressive, painfully nourishing
Air of a life which has run its course.
For I must go, I must go . . .

(*She goes out through the middle door.*)

CLAUDIO

Mother!

DEATH

Be still!

You cannot bring her back.

Claudio

Ah! Mother, come!
Let me but once with these quivering lips
Which, proud and tightly pressed, have always
Been silent, let me but so on my knees
Before you . . . Call her! Hold her back!
She did not wish to go! Did you not see?
Why, you monster, do you force her to go?

Death

Leave me what is mine. It *was* yours.

Claudio

Ah! and never
Felt! Barren, all is barren! When have I ever
Sensed that all the roots of my being
Strained towards her, that her presence,
Like the presence of a deity, filled me
With reverence and should replenish in me
Human longing, human joy and grief?

> (*Unconcerned with his lament, Death plays the melody
> of an old popular ballad. Slowly a young girl enters; she
> wears a plain flower-print dress, sandals, a piece of crape
> around the neck, her head bare.*)

The Young Girl

Yet it was beautiful . . . Do you never think of it?
Yes, though you caused me pain, oh, such pain . . .
But then, what is there that does not end in pain?
I have seen such few glad days, and these—
These were beautiful like a dream!
The flowers at the window, my flowers,
The little rickety spinet, the cabinet
In which I kept your letters and what

Gifts you may have given me . . . all that
—Do not laugh at me—all became beautiful
And spoke to me with ready loving lips!
When after a sultry evening the rain came down
And we stood by the window—ah, the fragrance
Of the dripping trees!—All that is gone;
What there was of life in it has died!
And lies in the small grave of our love.
Still, it was so beautiful, and you to blame
That it was so beautiful. And that afterwards
You flung me aside, careless, cruel, like a child,
Tired of playing, letting his flowers drop . . .
Oh God, I had nothing to hold you fast.

(Short pause)

And when your letter, the last hateful letter,
Came, I wished to die. Not to torment you
Do I tell you this. I wanted to write to you
To bid you farewell, without complaint,
Not violent, without wild grief; only so
That you might once again feel homesick
For my love and me, and weep a little
Because it was too late for that.
I did not write to you. No. What for?
Do I know how much of your heart was
In all that which filled my poor senses
So with splendor and fever that I walked
As in a dream in the broad light of day.
But kind intentions do not alter infidelity
And tears do not reawaken what has died away.
Besides, one does not die of it. Only much later,
After long and empty misery I might
Lie down to die. And I prayed that I
May be with you in your hour of death.
Not for the horror, not to torture you,

Only as when one drains a cup of wine
And the fragrance fleetingly reminds him
Of a faint pleasure somewhere left behind.

> (*She goes out; Claudio hides his face in his hands. As
> soon as she leaves a man comes in. He is approximately
> of Claudio's age. He wears an untidy, dust-covered
> traveling costume. In his left breast sticks a knife with a
> protruding wooden handle. He stops in the center of the
> stage, facing Claudio.*)

THE MAN

Are you still alive, perpetual trifler?
Still reading Horace and finding delight
In mocking-clever, never impassioned wit?
You came to me with fine words, stirred,
So it seemed, by what had also excited me . . .
I called things to mind, you said,
Which had slept inside you secretly,
As the nightwind sometimes speaks of distant ports. . .
O yes, were you not the strings of the lyre
Touched by the wind, and that amorous wind
Was always someone else's exploited breath,
Mine or another's. And for a very long time
We were friends. Friends? That is to say:
We shared, between us, conversation
Day and night, fellowship with the same
Young men, flirtation with the selfsame woman;
As master and slave share between them
House, chair, dog, dinner and whip:
The one thinks his house a pleasure, the other a jail;
One rides in the chair, the other's shoulder is galled
By the carved design; one lets his dog in the garden
Leap through hoops, the other must wait on him! . . .
Half-ripened feelings, my soul's pearls
Born in pain, you took from me

And tossed them like your plaything in the air.
You, quick to make friends, quickly done with each,
I with a dumb wooing in my soul
And with clenched teeth, you unblushingly
Touching everything, while for me the word,
Diffident and timid, died on the way.
Then a woman crossed our path. That which
Seized me, as one is seized by illness,
Where all one's senses reel, sleepless
From gazing too much at one mark . . .
At a mark so full of sweet sadness
And fierce brightness and fragrance, weaving
Like summer lightning out of deep darkness. . .
All that, you saw it too, it tempted you! . . .
"Because I am myself like that at times,
The girl's languid ways and harsh sublimity,
Such disillusionment and yet so young,
It tempted me." Did you not tell of it
Later in these words? It tempted you!
To me she was more than this blood and brain!
And weary of the sport you flung the toy to me,
Her whole image disfigured by your own
Weariness, so horribly distorted,
Stripped of her wonderful magic charm,
The features devoid of sense, the living hair
Hanging lifeless, a mask you flung at me,
Dissecting with loathsome skill the mystery
Of sweet grace into worthless dross.
For this I began to hate you at last as my dark
Premonition had always hated you,
And I avoided you.
                              Then I was driven by my fate
Which finally blessed my shattered life
With a purpose and a will in my heart—
For in your poisonous presence it had not

Wholly died to every impulse—
Yes, for a high cause my fate drove me
To the harsh death of a murderous blade,
Flinging me in a roadside ditch,
And lying there I slowly rotted
For things which you cannot comprehend,
And yet thrice blessed compared with you
Who meant nothing to anyone nor anyone to you.

(*He goes out.*)

CLAUDIO

True, nothing to anyone nor anyone to me.

(*Slowly raising himself*)

Like a poor player on the stage—
He enters on his cue, speaks his part and goes,
Indifferent towards all else, listless,
Unmoved by the sounds of his own voice
And dull of tone, never moving others:
Thus have I walked across this stage
Of life, worthless and powerless.
Why did this happen to me? Why, Death,
Must I learn from you to see life
Passing thus before me, not through a veil,
Sharp and whole, awakening something here?
Why is it that such deep foreknowledge of the things
Of life takes possession of the childish mind
That afterwards the things when they are real
Bring only the stale flurry of remembrance?
Why does not your violin resound for us,
Casting up the hidden spirit world,
Which our bosom secretly contains,
Buried deep, so sealed from consciousness,
As flowers lie buried under rubble and earth?
Oh, that I could be near you, where

You can be heard untroubled by pettiness!
I can! Grant me what you have threatened:
Since my life was death, then, Death, be my life!
What compels me, who know not either,
To call you Death and the other Life?
Into one hour you can compress of life
More than my whole life could comprise;
I will forget all that was shadowy
And devote myself to your miracles and powers.

(He reflects for a moment.)

Perhaps this is only a dying reflection,
Washed up by the deadly wakeful blood,
Yet have I never with all my living senses
Perceived so much, and so I call it good!
If I must now, extinguished, sink down and die
And my brain is thus full of this hour,
Then let all pale life vanish away:
For only as I die I feel that I am.
When one is dreaming, an excess of
Dreamt feeling can cause him to wake,
So now, in an excess of feeling, I seem to awake
From life's dream in death's wakefulness.

(He sinks down dead at Death's feet.)

DEATH

(As he slowly goes out shaking his head)

How marvelous these creatures are,
Who explain what is inexplicable,
Read what has never been written,
Master confusion and set it right
And still find ways in the eternal night.

*(He disappears through the middle door; his words fade
away.)*

(In the room all remains silent. Through the window one sees Death passing by outside playing the violin; behind him the Mother, also the Girl, and close to them a figure resembling Claudio.)

Electra

A Tragedy in One Act
Freely Rendered after Sophocles

Characters

The inner courtyard, bounded by the rear wall of the palace and low buildings in which the servants live. Women servants at the well, left front. Among them matron overseers.

FIRST SERVANT

lifting her water pitcher

What's become of Electra?

SECOND SERVANT

Why, it's her hour,
her time of day when she howls for her father
so that the walls resound.

Electra comes running from the hallway which is already growing dark. All turn to look at her. Electra bounds back like an animal into its hiding place, holding one arm in front of her face.

69

FIRST SERVANT

Did you see how she looked at us?

SECOND SERVANT

Spiteful
like a wild cat.

THIRD SERVANT

Not long ago she lay there
and groaned—

FIRST SERVANT

Always when the sun goes down
she lies there and groans.

THIRD SERVANT

And two of us went by
and came too close to her—

FIRST SERVANT

She cannot bear it
if you look at her.

THIRD SERVANT

Yes, we came
too close to her. She spit like a cat
at us. "Off with you, flies!" she yelled, "Off!"

FOURTH SERVANT

"Blowflies, off with you!"

THIRD SERVANT

"Don't settle on my wounds!"
and struck at us with a whisk.

FOURTH SERVANT

"Off with you,
blowflies, begone!"

THIRD SERVANT

"I won't have you glut
on the sweets of my pain; nor relish the foam
of my writhing lips."

FOURTH SERVANT

"Begone, crawl away and hide,"
she yelled after us. "Eat fat things and sweet things
and creep into bed with your men," she cried,
and this one here—

THIRD SERVANT

I didn't mince my words—

FOURTH SERVANT

She answered her!

THIRD SERVANT

I did: "When you are hungry," I answered her,
"you also eat," and she sprang to her feet and shot
horrible looks at us; she stretched her fingers
like claws at us and screamed: "I'm feeding,"
she screamed, "I'm feeding a vulture in my body."

SECOND SERVANT

And you?

THIRD SERVANT

"That's why you always squat," I told her,
"where the smell of carrion holds you and scrape
for an ancient corpse!"

SECOND SERVANT

And what did she say
to that?

THIRD SERVANT

She broke into howls and threw herself
in her corner.

They have finished drawing water from the well.

FIRST SERVANT

That the queen allows
such a demon foot-loose to play her tricks
all through the house.

SECOND SERVANT

And her own child, too!

FIRST SERVANT

If she were mine, I'd keep her—by God, I would!—
under lock and key.

FOURTH SERVANT

Are they not harsh enough
with her? Do they not set her bowl of food
down among the dogs?

Softly

Haven't you ever seen
the master beat her?

FIFTH SERVANT

a very young girl, with a trembling excited voice

I will throw myself
down before her and I will kiss her feet.

Is she not a royal child and suffers
such disgrace! I will anoint her feet
and dry them with my hair.

MATRON

Inside with you!

Pushes her.

FIFTH SERVANT

There is nothing in the world that is nobler
than she. She lies in rags stretched out
on the threshold, but there is no one,

Shouting

there is no one in this house who can endure
her look!

MATRON

Inside!

Pushes her through the low open door on the left, front.

FIFTH SERVANT

caught in the door

None of you is worthy
to breathe the air which she is breathing! Oh,
if I could see you strangled, see you all
in a dark shed hanging by your necks,
for what you have done to Electra!

MATRON

slams the door shut and stands with her back against it

Do you hear? what we
have done to Electra! who pushed her bowl from our

table, when she was told to eat with us,
who spat at our feet and called us bitches.

FIRST SERVANT

What? She said: *no* dog can be degraded
to do what we were trained to do: to wash
with water and with more and more fresh-drawn
water the everlasting blood of murder
off the floors—

THIRD SERVANT

And sweep the shame, she said,
the shame which renews itself by day and night
into the corners . . .

FIRST SERVANT

Our body, so she cries,
bristles with the filth which we are forced to serve!

They carry their pitchers into the house, left.

MATRON

who has opened the door for them

And when she sees us with our children, she screams:
nothing can be so accursed, nothing,
as children which, like animals, slithering about
in blood on the stairs, we have conceived and born
here in this house. Does she say these things
or not?

THE SERVANTS

from inside

Yes! yes!

One of them

from inside

They are beating me!

The matron goes inside. The door closes.
Electra comes out of the house. She is alone with the patches of red light which fall like bloodstains from the branches of the fig tree obliquely across the ground and upon the walls.

Electra

Alone! Ah! all alone. My father is gone,
driven away, down into his cold pit.

Toward the ground

Where are you, father? do you not have
the strength to lift up your face towards me?
It is the time, it is our time!
It is the hour in which they butchered you,
your wife and he that sleeps with her
in one bed, your royal bed.
They struck you in the bath, your blood
ran over your eyes, and the bath
steamed with your blood; then he seized you,
the coward, by your shoulders, dragged you
out of the room, head first, the feet
trailing behind: your eyes, wide open,
stared fixedly into the house.
And thus you come again, setting one foot
before the other, and suddenly you stand there,
with wide-open eyes and around your forehead
a royal wreath of purple which feeds
upon the open wound of your head.

Father!

I want to see you, leave me not alone today!
Even if only like yesterday, like a shadow,
there by the wall show yourself to your child!
Father! your day will come! From the stars
all time comes rushing down, so will the blood
from a hundred throats rush down upon your grave!
As from upturned jugs it will flow
from the shackled murderers, and roundabout
like marble jugs will be the naked bodies
of all their helpers, of men and women,
and in one flood, in a swelling stream,
their life's life will rush out of them—
and we will slaughter the steeds for you
which are in the house, we will drive them together
before your grave, and they will sense their death
beforehand and neigh into the wind of death
and die, and we will slaughter the dogs for you
because they are the brood and the brood of the brood
of those who have hunted with you, of those
who licked your feet, to whom you flung
morsels of meat, therefore their blood
must go down to do you service, and we,
your blood, your son Orestes and your daughters,
we three, when all this is done and purple tents
have been raised by the haze of the blood
which the sun sucks upward to itself, then
we, your blood, will dance around your grave:
and above the dead men I will lift my knee
high in the air, step by step, and they
who will see me dance, yes, even they
who will see my shadow only from afar
dancing so, they will say: for a great king
this royal pageantry is being held
by his flesh and blood, and happy is he

who has children that dance such royal dances
of victory around his noble grave!

CHRYSOTHEMIS

*the younger sister, stands in the doorway of the house. She
looks fearfully at Electra, calls softly*

Electra!

*Electra starts like a sleepwalker who hears his name called.
She staggers. Her eyes look about as if they did not at once
discern anything. Her face is contorted as she sees the frightened face of her sister.*

Chrysothemis stands pressed to the door.

ELECTRA

Ah, that face!

CHRYSOTHEMIS

Is my face so hateful to you?

ELECTRA

What do you want? Speak up, pour out your speech,
then go and let me be!

Chrysothemis raises her hands as if warding off a blow.

ELECTRA

Why do *you* lift your hands?
Thus, father lifted both his hands,
then the axe fell and split his flesh.
What do you want, daughter of my mother?

CHRYSOTHEMIS

They are plotting something dreadful.

77

ELECTRA

The two women?

CHRYSOTHEMIS

Who?

ELECTRA

Why, my mother
and that other woman, aye, that milksop,
Aegisthus, that brave murderer, he
who does heroic deeds only in bed.
Well, what are they plotting?

CHRYSOTHEMIS

They will throw you
into a dungeon where you cannot see
the light of sun and moon.

Electra laughs.

CHRYSOTHEMIS

They will do it,
I know, I heard it.

ELECTRA

I feel as if *I* had heard it.
Was it not at table, and over the last dish?
Then he likes to raise his voice and boast,
I think it helps his digestion.

CHRYSOTHEMIS

Not at table.
Not to boast. He and she, alone
they talk of it.

ELECTRA

Alone? Then how could you
have heard it?

CHRYSOTHEMIS

At the door, Electra.

ELECTRA

Open no doors in this house! Faugh!
Choked breathing, faugh! and the death rattle
of strangled men, there's nothing else here
in all these rooms. No, leave alone the door
behind which you hear a groan: for they're not always
killing, sometimes they are alone together!
Open no doors! Do not sneak about.
Sit on the ground like me and wish for
death and judgment upon her and him.

CHRYSOTHEMIS

I cannot sit and stare into the dark
like you. As though I had a fire inside me,
I am driven constantly about this house,
I cannot bear to stay in any room,
I must be running from door to door, oh!
upstairs and down again, as if a voice
were calling me, and when I come, an empty
room stares at me. I am so afraid,
my knees are trembling by day and night,
my throat is choked, I cannot even weep,
all has turned to stone! Sister, have pity!

ELECTRA

On whom?

CHRYSOTHEMIS

It is you who rivet me to the ground
with iron bolts. If it were not for you,
they would let us out. But for your smouldering hatred,
your sleepless and ungovernable mind,
at which they tremble, they would let us out
of this prison, sister! I want to get out!
I do not want to sleep here every night
until I die! Before I die I also
want to live! I want to bring forth children
before my body withers, and were it a peasant
to whom they give me, I will bear him children,
and warm them with my body in the cold nights
when gales beat down the shack! But this
I cannot endure any longer, loitering here
with household servants, yet not their equal,
shut in by day and night with my mortal terror!
Are you listening? Speak to me, sister!

ELECTRA

Poor
creature!

CHRYSOTHEMIS

Have pity on yourself and me. Who profits
by this anguish? Our father perhaps?
Our father is dead. Our brother is not
coming home. You can see that he will not come.
With knives each passing day carves his mark
on your face and mine, and outside, the sun rises
and sets, and women whom I have known slender
are heavy with blessing, and toil on their way
to the well and scarcely lift the pail, and all
at once they are delivered of their weight

and come to the well again and they themselves
flow with sweet drink, and, suckling, a new life
clings to them, and the children grow—
but we sit always here on our perch
like fettered birds, turning our heads
to left and right, and no one comes, no brother,
no messenger from our brother, not even
a messenger's messenger, nothing! Better dead
than live and yet not live. No, I am
a woman and I desire a woman's fate.

ELECTRA

Fie,
the woman who thinks of it, who calls it by name!
To be the cave the murderer enjoys
after the murder; to play the beast giving
pleasure to the fouler beast. Ah, with one
she sleeps, presses her breasts on his two eyes
and beckons to the other who creeps from behind
the bed with axe and net.

CHRYSOTHEMIS

You are horrible!

ELECTRA

Why horrible? Are you such a woman?
You only want to become one.

CHRYSOTHEMIS

Can you not
forget? My head is always confused. I can
remember nothing from today until tomorrow.
Sometimes I lie there, and then I am what I was
before, and cannot understand that I am
no longer young. What, what has become of it all?

For it is not water which is rushing by,
and it is not yarn which is rolling off,
rolling off the spool; it is I, I!
I would pray that a god might kindle a light
in my breast, that I might find myself again
inside myself! If I were gone from here,
how quickly I would forget all bad dreams—

ELECTRA

Forget? What! am I a beast? forget?
The brute beast falls asleep, the half-devoured
prey still dangling from the lip, the brute forgets
and begins to chew while death already sits
on it and throttles it; the beast forgets
what crept out of its body, and stills its hunger
with its own child—I am no beast, *I cannot
forget!*

CHRYSOTHEMIS

Oh, must my soul forever eat
of this food which it loathes, which it
so loathes! to smell it only makes it
shudder; never, never should it have
touched it; never, never should it have
known that such a gruesome thing exists,
never known! never seen with eyes! never heard!
Such dreadful things are not for the heart
of man! When it comes, when it shows
itself, one must flee from the houses, flee
into the vineyards, flee into the mountains!
and if it climb the mountains, one must again
come down and creep away into the houses:
never must one abide with it, never
remain in one house with it! I must get out!
I want to conceive and bear children who know

nothing of this; I will wash my body
in every water; I will plunge deep down
into every water; I will wash each
part of me; the hollows of my eyes
I will wash clean—they must not be frightened
when they look into their mother's eyes!

ELECTRA

scornfully

When they look into their mother's eyes!
And how do you look into father's eyes?

CHRYSOTHEMIS

Stop it!

ELECTRA

May your children, when you have them,
do to you as you have done to your father!

Chrysothemis bursts into tears.

What are you wailing for? Be off! In with you!
There is your place. I hear a noise inside.
Are they perhaps preparing your wedding feast
for you? I hear them run. The whole house
is up. They labor in childbirth or
they murder. When they have no corpses
to sleep upon, they must needs murder!

CHRYSOTHEMIS

Stop it. All that is past. Stop!

ELECTRA

Past? In there it is beginning again!
Do you think I do not know the sound as they
drag dead men down the stairs, as they whisper
and wring out linen full of blood?

CHRYSOTHEMIS

Sister!
Go away from here.

ELECTRA

This time I want to be present!
Not like that other time. This time I am strong.
I will throw myself upon her, I will snatch
the axe from her hand and swing it above her—

CHRYSOTHEMIS

Go away, hide yourself! that she may not see you.
Do not stand in her way this day; there is
death in her every look. She has been dreaming.

Inside, the noise of numerous people approaching, coming nearer.

Go away from here. They come through the corridor.
They are passing by here. She has been dreaming:
I don't know what, I heard it from the servants,
I don't know whether it is true, sister:
they say that she has dreamed of Orestes,
and that she cried out loud in her sleep
as one cries out who is being strangled.

ELECTRA

I! I!
I sent it to her. From out of my breast
I visited this dream upon her! I lie
and hear the steps of him who looks for her.
I hear him walk through the rooms, I hear him
raise the curtain from the bed: screaming
she escapes, but he is after her:
the hunt is on, down the stairs
through vaults, vaults upon vaults.

It is much darker than night, much quieter
and darker than the grave, she pants and staggers
in the darkness, but he is after her:
he waves the torch in his left, in his right the axe.
And I am like a dog upon her heels:
if she tries to run into a cave, I leap
at her from the side, thus we drive her on
until a wall blocks everything, and there,
in the deepest darkness, yet I see him well,
a shade, and yet limbs and yet the white
of one eye, there sits our father:
he does not heed it and yet it must be done:
in front of his feet we press her down,
and the axe falls!

*Torches and human figures fill the passageway to the
left of the door.*

CHRYSOTHEMIS

They are coming. She drives all the servants
with torches before her. They drag animals
behind them and the sacrificial knives. Sister,
when she trembles, she is most terrible; if only
this day, only this hour, go out of her way!

ELECTRA

I am in the mood to speak with my mother
as never before!

*A hurried procession passes the glaringly lit-up windows
clanking and shuffling by: it is a tugging and dragging of animals, a muted scolding, a quickly stifled scream, the whistling
sound of a whip, a recovering and staggering onward.*

CHRYSOTHEMIS

I do not want to hear it.

Rushes out through the courtyard door.
The figure of Clytemnestra appears in the wide window.

*Her pale, puffed-up face in the glaring light of the torches
appears even paler above the scarlet robe. She supports herself on the arm of a confidante, who is dressed in dark violet,
and on an ivory staff adorned with jewels. A yellow figure,
with black hair which is combed straight back, resembling
an Egyptian woman, with a smooth face, like an upright
snake, carries her train. The queen is completely covered
with jewels and charms. Her arms are covered with arm
bands, her fingers bristle with rings. The lids of her eyes
seem excessively large, and it appears to be a terrible effort
for her to keep them open.*

*Electra stands rigidly upright, her face turned towards
this window.*

*Clytemnestra opens her eyes suddenly, and trembling
with anger she steps to the edge of the window and points
with her staff at Electra.*

CLYTEMNESTRA

at the window

What do you want? Look, my women! Look, there!
How it rears up with swelling neck
and darts its tongue at me! and that
I let run free in my own house!
If she could kill me with her looks!
O gods, why do you thus bear down on me?
Why do you ravage me? why must
my strength be lame inside me, why is
my living body like a waste field,
and this nettle growing out of me,
and I do not have the strength to weed!
Why does this happen to me, you eternal gods?

ELECTRA

Gods! but you are yourself a goddess!
You are what they are.

Clytemnestra

Did you hear? did you
understand what she speaks?

The Confidante

That you are also
of the race of the gods.

The Trainbearer

hissing

She means it maliciously.

Clytemnestra

as her heavy eyelids shut

It sounds so familiar. And only as if
I had forgotten it, long long ago.
She knows me well. Yet one can never know
what she is plotting secretly.

*The Confidante and the Trainbearer whisper with
one another.*

Electra

You are no longer yourself. These reptiles
always hang about you. What they hiss
into your ear tears your thinking forever
in two; and so you go about in a frenzy,
you are always as in a dream.

Clytemnestra

I will come down.
Let be, I wish to speak with her. She is
not loathsome today. She speaks like a physician.
The hours hold all things in their direction.

Each and every thing can first be frightful,
then turn its pleasant face towards us.

*She leaves the window and appears in the door, the
Confidante at her side, the Trainbearer behind her, torches
behind them.*

CLYTEMNESTRA

from the threshold

Why do you call me a goddess? Do you speak so
out of spite? Take care. This day could be
the last day that you may see this light
and that you may breathe this free air.

ELECTRA

Truly, if you are not a goddess,
then where are gods! I know of nothing
in the world which makes me shudder except to think
that this body is the dark door through which
I crept into the light of this world.
Did I lie upon this lap, naked?
Did you lift me to these breasts?
Why, then I crept out of my father's grave
and played in swaddling clothes upon
my father's scaffold! Why, you are
a colossus from whose iron hands
I have never escaped. You keep a tight rein
on me. You tether me to what you will.
You have spewed out for me, like the sea,
a life, a father, brother and sister:
and swallowed down, like the sea,
a life, a father, brother and sister.
I know not how I should ever perish—
except of this, that you should perish too.

CLYTEMNESTRA

You do me such honor? Is there yet
something of piety left in you?

ELECTRA

                              Much! Much!
What weighs heavy on your heart also
touches mine. You see, it grieves me
to see Aegisthus, your husband, wearing
the old robes of my dead father, you know,
the former king. Indeed, it grieves my heart:
I think they do not suit him. I think
they are too wide around his chest.

THE CONFIDANTE

                              She says not
what she means.

THE TRAINBEARER

Each word is false.

CLYTEMNESTRA

angry

I will not listen to you. What comes from you
is only the breath of Aegisthus. I will not
find fault with everything. If she speaks
to me what I am glad to hear, then I will listen
to what she speaks. What the truth is
no man can find out. No one on earth
knows the truth about things that are hidden.
Are there not some in the dungeons who say
that I am a murderess and that
Aegisthus is a common assassin?
And when I wake you in the night, do you

not each say something different? Do you not
cry that my eyelids are swollen and that
my liver is sick, and that everything
comes only from the sick liver, and you,
do you not whine into the other ear
that you have seen demons with long pointed
bills that suck my blood? Do you not show me
the marks on my flesh, and do I not
obey you and slaughter, slaughter, slaughter
victim upon victim? Do you not rip me to death
with your pleas and counterpleas? I do not want
to hear any longer: this is true and this a lie.
If anyone says pleasant things to me,
and were it my daughter, were it that one there,
I will loosen the covers from my soul and let
the soft breeze in wherever it may come,
as do the sick when in the evening, sitting
by the pond, they uncover to the cool breeze
their boils and all their festering parts, sitting
in the cool breeze of evening and thinking of nothing
except to find relief. So now will I
for once begin to look after myself.
Leave me alone with her.

Impatiently she directs the Confidante and the Train-
bearer with her staff to go into the house. They disappear,
hesitating at the door. Also the torches disappear, and only
from the inside of the house a faint light falls through the
corridor into the yard and touches now and then the figures
of the two women.

CLYTEMNESTRA

after a pause

I do not have good nights. Have you
no remedy for dreams?

ELECTRA

moving closer

Do you dream, mother?

CLYTEMNESTRA

Have you no other words to comfort me?
Loosen your tongue. Yes, yes, I dream.
As one gets older, one dreams. Yet it can be
dispelled. Why are you standing there in the dark?
We need only make subservient to us
the powers that are scattered somewhere. There are
rites. There must be proper rites for everything.
How one pronounces a word, and a sentence,
much depends on that. Also on the hour.
And whether one is full, or fasting. Many a man
has perished because he stepped into the bath
at the wrong hour.

ELECTRA

Are you now thinking
of my father?

CLYTEMNESTRA

That is why I am covered
so with gems. For there dwells in each of them
a power, I am sure. One need only know
how to use it. If only you were willing,
you could say something that is of help to me.

ELECTRA

I, mother, I?

CLYTEMNESTRA

Yes, you! for you are clever.
In your head there is great skill. You speak

of old events as if they had happened
yesterday. But I—I rot inside.
I think, but it all mounts up in me,
one thing on top of another. I open my mouth,
and Aegisthus screams, and what he screams fills me
with hatred; I want to rear up and be stronger
than his words—and I find nothing,
I find nothing! Suddenly I do not know
if he had said today what makes me tremble
with wrath, whether today or another time,
once long ago; then I am giddy, suddenly
I do not know any longer who I am,
and that is the horror of sinking alive
into chaos, and Aegisthus! Aegisthus,
he mocks me, and I find nothing, I do not find
the terrible things before which he would
have to be silent and, pale like myself, stare
into the fire. But you possess the words.
You could say much that would be of help to me.
Even though a word is nothing at all! For what is
a breath! And yet between night and day,
when I lie with open eyes, something there is
that creeps over me, it is no word, it is
no pain, it does not press, it does not strangle me,
it lets me lie there as I am and here
at my side lies Aegisthus, and there,
there is the curtain: everything looks at me
as if from eternity to eternity:
it is nothing, not even a nightmare, and yet
it is so terrible that my soul
wishes it were hanged and every limb
of mine yearns for death, and yet I live
and am not even sick: as you can see:
do I look sick? Is it then possible
to perish, alive, like a rotting carcass?

Can one waste away and not be sick?
go to wrack, with waking senses, like a robe
eaten up by moths? And then I sleep
and dream, and dream! So that the marrow dissolves
in my bones, and stagger to my feet again,
and not the tenth part of the water clock
has run out, and that which grins at me underneath
the curtain is not yet the pale morning,
no, it is still the torch before the door,
which flickers frightfully like a living thing
and spies on my sleep.
I do not know who they are that do this
to me, and if they dwell above or somewhere
down below—when I see *you* standing there
as now, I think you must have a part in this.
But then, what are you? You do not even know
how to say one word when one listens to you.
Whom could it profit or harm at all
whether you live or not? Why do you stare
at me so? I will not allow you to look
at me so. But these dreams must have
an end. Whoever it may be that sends them:
any demon will let go of us
as soon as the right blood has flowed.

ELECTRA

> Any demon!

CLYTEMNESTRA

And if I had to bleed every beast
that creeps and flies, and rise and go to sleep
in the steam of the blood, like the people
of the farthest Thule in the blood-red fog:
I will no longer dream.

93

ELECTRA

When the right
victim falls beneath the axe, you will
no longer dream.

CLYTEMNESTRA

stepping closer to her

You know then with which
consecrated beast—

ELECTRA

One that is not consecrated!

CLYTEMNESTRA

Which is tied up, inside?

ELECTRA

No! it runs free.

CLYTEMNESTRA

eagerly

And what sort of rites?

ELECTRA

Wonderful rites,
and to be strictly performed.

CLYTEMNESTRA

Speak up!

ELECTRA

Can you not guess?

CLYTEMNESTRA

No, that is why I ask.
Say the name of the victim.

ELECTRA

A woman.

CLYTEMNESTRA

eagerly

One of my serving women, speak!
a child? a young virgin? a woman
already known by man?

ELECTRA

Yes! known!
that's it!

CLYTEMNESTRA

And how sacrificed? what hour?
and where?

ELECTRA

In any place, at any hour
of the day or the night.

CLYTEMNESTRA

Reveal the rites!
How would I perform them? I must myself—

ELECTRA

No.
This time you do not hunt with net and axe.

CLYTEMNESTRA

Who else? who does it?

ELECTRA

A man

CLYTEMNESTRA

Aegisthus?

ELECTRA

laughs

I said: a man!

CLYTEMNESTRA

Who? answer me.
Someone from this house? or must a stranger
come?

ELECTRA

gazing vacantly on the ground, absent-minded

Yes, yes, a stranger. But still
he is of this house.

CLYTEMNESTRA

Do not pose riddles for me.
Electra, listen to me. I am glad
that today I find you for once not stubborn.
When parents are harsh it is always the child
who forces them to be so. No strict word
is quite irrevocable, and the mother,
when she sleeps badly, thinks rather of her child
lying in the marriage bed than on a chain.

ELECTRA

in an undertone

The opposite of the child: who would rather
think the mother dead than in her bed.

CLYTEMNESTRA

What are you mumbling? I say that no thing
is irrevocable. For do not all things
turn before our eyes and change like fog?
And *we*, we ourselves! and our deeds!
Deeds! We and deeds! What odd words!
For am I still the same who has done the deed?
And if so! done, done! done! what a word
to throw in my teeth! There he stood
of whom you always talk, there he stood
and here stood I and there Aegisthus,
and from eye to eye our glances met:
so it had not happened yet! and then
your father's dying look altered
so slowly and horribly, but still
fastened to mine—and then it had happened:
there is no space between! Now it was
before, and then it was past—in between
I did nothing.

ELECTRA

No, the work that lay between
the axe had done alone.

CLYTEMNESTRA

How you thrust in
the words.

ELECTRA

Not so skilled nor so fast
as you the strokes of the axe.

CLYTEMNESTRA

I do not want
to hear of it. Be silent. If I met
your father today—as I am speaking here
to you, so could I speak with him. Maybe
I would shudder, but it may also be
that I could speak tenderly and weep
as when two old friends happen to meet.

ELECTRA

in an undertone

Horrible, she speaks of the murder as if it were
a quarrel before supper.

CLYTEMNESTRA

Tell your sister
she should not flee before me like a frightened dog
into the darkness. Tell her to greet me
cheerfully, as is becoming, and answer me
calmly. Then I would truly have no cause
to hinder me from giving you and her
in marriage before the winter.

ELECTRA

And our brother?
Will you not let him come home, mother?

CLYTEMNESTRA

I have forbidden you to speak of him.

ELECTRA

Then you fear him?

CLYTEMNESTRA

Who says that?

ELECTRA

Why, mother,
you are trembling!

CLYTEMNESTRA

Who would fear
a feeble-minded boy?

ELECTRA

What?

CLYTEMNESTRA

They say
he stammers, sprawls in the yard among the dogs
and cannot tell man and beast apart.

ELECTRA

The child was perfectly well.

CLYTEMNESTRA

They say they gave him
a wretched place to live and the barnyard
animals for company.

ELECTRA

Ah!

CLYTEMNESTRA

with lowered eyelids

I sent
much gold and yet more gold that they might
keep him like a royal child.

ELECTRA

You lie!
You sent the gold that they might strangle him.

CLYTEMNESTRA

Who tells you that?

ELECTRA

I see it in your eyes.
But by your trembling I also see that he
is still alive. That you think of nothing
by day and night except of him. That your heart
is withering for fear, because you know: he comes.

CLYTEMNESTRA

Do not lie. Anyone outside this house
does not concern me. I live here and I am
mistress. Servants I have enough to guard
the doors, and if I wish I will have three
armed guards sit with open eyes by day and night
before my room. I do not even hear
what you say. Nor do I know who he is
of whom you speak. I will never see him:
what is it to me to know if he is
alive or not? To say it quite plainly,
I have had enough of dreaming about him.
Dreams are unwholesome, they waste our strength,
and I wish to live and be the mistress here.

I do not want to have such fitful spells
as to stand here like a market woman
and to tell you of my nights. I am
as good as sick, and sick men gossip .
of their ills, that is all. But I will
not be sick any longer. And in one way

She raises her staff threateningly towards Electra

or another I will force the right word
from your lips. Already you have betrayed
yourself saying you know the right victim
and also the rites that will help me. If you
will not speak being free, you will on the chain.
If not, being full, then you will speak from hunger.
One can get rid of dreams. He who suffers
from them and does not find the means to get
relief is only a fool. I will find out
who must bleed so I can sleep again.

ELECTRA

with a leap out of the darkness, coming steadily closer towards her, rising up, more and more terrible

What must bleed? Your own neck must bleed
when the hunter has moved in for the kill!
He will knife his game: but only on the run!
Who'd slaughter a victim in sleep! He'll hunt you up,
he'll drive you through the house! If you go to the right,
there stands the bed! to the left, there foams the bath
like blood! the darkness and the torches cast
red-black death nets over you—

Clytemnestra, shaken with voiceless fear, tries to run into the house. Electra hauls her by her dress to the front. Clytemnestra draws back against the wall. Her eyes are wide open, the staff drops from her trembling hands.

101

You want to cry out, but the air stifles
the unborn cry and lets it drop to the ground
silently; as if out of your senses, you offer
the nape of your neck, and you feel the sharp edge
plunging into the seat of life, but he
holds back the stroke: the rites have not yet been fulfilled.
He draws you by the tresses of your hair,
and all is silent, you hear your own heart
beating against your ribs: this space of time
—it spreads before you like a dark abyss
of years—this time is given to you
to guess how shipwrecked men do feel
when the blackness of clouds and death corrodes
their useless cries; the time is given to you
to envy all those who are fettered with chains
to dungeon walls, who on the bottom of wells
cry out for death as for their deliverer—
for you, you lie imprisoned in your own
self as if it were the glowing hot belly
of a brazen beast—and, just as now,
you cannot cry out! And I stand next to you:
you cannot turn your eyes away from me,
for you are tortured with convulsive desire
to read one word upon my silent face,
you roll your eyes, you want to think
of anything, grinning you want to lure the gods
down from the cloudy skies of the night:
the gods are having supper! As at the time
when you slaughtered my father, they sit
at supper and are deaf to choking throats!
Only a half-mad god, Laughter, he staggers
in by the door: he thinks you are dallying
with Aegisthus at loving time; but
instantly he notes his error, laughs
his shrill laugh and is gone at once.

Then you also have enough. Your gall trickles
bitter drops into your heart, expiring
you want to recollect one word, to utter
only one word, any word, instead of
the tear of blood which even the beast
is not denied in death: but I stand there
before you, and then you read with a fixed
eye the monstrous word that is written
upon my face: for my face is mingled
of my father's features and of yours,
and so with my standing there in silence
I have utterly destroyed your last word;
hanged is your soul in the noose twisted
by yourself, the axe now whistles through the air,
and I stand there and see you die at last!
Then you will never dream again, then I need
dream no longer, and he who then is still
alive can shout with joy over his life!

*They stand face to face, Electra in the wildest intoxica-
tion, Clytemnestra breathing harshly with fear. At this moment the hallway becomes bright, and the Confidante comes
running out. She whispers something in Clytemnestra's ear;
but at first she does not seem to understand. Gradually she
collects herself. She beckons: lights! Servants with torches
come out and stand behind Clytemnestra. She beckons: more
lights! More women come out and take their stand behind her
so that the courtyard becomes bright with lights and a red-
yellow glare floods the walls. Now the features of Clytemnestra's face gradually change, and the tension of her terror
gives way to an expression of evil triumph. She demands to
hear the whispered message again and meanwhile does not
let Electra for a moment out of her sight. Glutting herself
with a savage joy, she stretches both hands menacingly
against Electra. Then the Confidante picks up the staff for
her, and Clytemnestra, leaning on both, hurriedly, eagerly,*

*gathering up her robes on the steps, runs into the house.
The servants with the lights rush behind her as if pursued.*

ELECTRA

in the meantime

What are they saying to her? why look, she is glad!
O my head! I can't think why. What gives such joy
to the woman?

*Chrysothemis enters by the courtyard door, running,
howling loudly like a wounded animal.*

ELECTRA

Chrysothemis! Quick, quick,
I need your help. Name something in this world
that can give one joy!

CHRYSOTHEMIS

shrieking

Orestes! Orestes
is dead!

ELECTRA

warns her off; as if out of her senses

Be still!

CHRYSOTHEMIS

close by her

Orestes is dead!

Electra moves her lips.

CHRYSOTHEMIS

I came outside, they knew it already! They all
stood about, and all knew it, only we
did not.

ELECTRA

No one knows it.

CHRYSOTHEMIS

All know it!

ELECTRA

No one can know it: because it is not true.

Chrysothemis throws herself on the ground.

ELECTRA

pulls her up

It is not true! I tell you! I say to you,
it is not true!

CHRYSOTHEMIS

The strangers stood by the wall, the strangers
who are sent here to bring the message: two of them,
an old man and a young man. They had already
told it to every one. All stood around them
in a circle and all knew it already.

ELECTRA

It is not true.

CHRYSOTHEMIS

Only we are not told!
No one thinks of us. Dead! Electra, dead!

A Young Manservant

comes hurrying out of the house, stumbles over the form lying before the threshold.

Make room here! who's loafing here before a door?
Ah, I might have known! Ho there, stableboy! Hey!

The Cook

comes through the door, right

What is the matter?

The Young Servant

    I split my lungs calling
for a stableboy, and who crawls out of his hole—
the cook.

An Old Servant

with a dour face, appears at the courtyard door.

What do you want at the stables?

The Young Servant

         Saddle up,
as quick as you can! do you hear?
A nag, a mule, or a cow for all I care,
but be quick about it!

The Old Servant

For whom?

The Young Servant

       For the fellow
who tells you. Now he stands there and gapes! Quick,
for me! Right now! One, two! One, two! For I must
ride out in the fields and bring the master home,

because I have a message for him, great news,
important enough to ride one of your mares
to death.

The old servant disappears.

THE COOK

What sort of news? Say
a word or two!

THE YOUNG SERVANT

A word or two, my dear cook,
would probably be of no use to you. Besides,
it would be hard to sum up in one word
and plainly what I know and what I have to
report to the master: let you be satisfied
when you are told that a message has just arrived
here in the house of the utmost importance
—how long such an old bag of bones takes
to saddle a horse!—which, as a loyal servant
of this household ought to delight you: whether
you know what it is or not, all the same,
it has to delight you.

Roaring into the yard

A whip, you scoundrel! what,
do you think I'll ride him without a whip? You,
it's you keep me waiting, not I the nag!

To the Cook, on the point of leaving

Well, in a word: the young fellow Orestes,
the son of the house, who was always away
from home, and therefore as good as dead:
in short, this fellow, who after all has, so to speak,
been always dead, is now, so to speak, really dead!

Rushes off.

The Cook

*in the direction of Electra and Chrysothemis, who lie
there pressed close to one another, like one body which is
shaken by the sobs of Chrysothemis and above which rises
the deathly pale silent face of Electra*

Eh! now I have found it out! The dogs howl
with the full moon, and you howl because now
it is always new moon for you. The dogs are driven
away when they disturb the peace of the house.
Be on your guard, or it will happen to you.

Goes in again.

Chrysothemis

halfway rising

Perished in a foreign land! dead! buried
there away from home. Killed by his horses
and dragged along the ground! Ah, his face
unrecognizable, they say. We have never
seen it, his face! When we think of him,
we think of a child. And he was tall.
I wonder did he ask for us before
he died! I could not question them:
everybody stood around them. Electra,
we must go up and speak with these men.

Electra

in an undertone

Now it must be done by us.

Chrysothemis

Electra,
let us go there: they are two, an old one
and one much younger; when they find out

that we are the sisters, his poor sisters,
they will tell us all.

ELECTRA

What good is it
to know more? That he is dead we know.

CHRYSOTHEMIS

Ah, to have brought us nothing, not even
a lock of hair, not one small lock of hair!
As if we were no longer among the living,
we two girls.

ELECTRA

Therefore we must now show
that we are.

CHRYSOTHEMIS

Electra?

ELECTRA

Yes, we!
We two must do it.

CHRYSOTHEMIS

Electra, what?

ELECTRA

It were best, today, and best, this night.

CHRYSOTHEMIS

What, sister?

ELECTRA

What? the work that has now
fallen to us, because he cannot come
and, yet, it must not remain undone.

CHRYSOTHEMIS

What work?

ELECTRA

Now you and I must go
and kill the woman and her spouse.

CHRYSOTHEMIS

Sister, do you speak of our mother?

ELECTRA

Of her. And also of him. It must be done
without delay.

Chrysothemis is speechless.

ELECTRA

Keep still. There is nothing to say.
Nothing to consider except: how?
how we will do it.

CHRYSOTHEMIS

I?

ELECTRA

Yes, you and I.
Who else? Has our father other children
hidden somewhere in the house who could
come to our aid? No, as far as I know.

CHRYSOTHEMIS

We two must go and do this? We? we two?
with our two hands?

ELECTRA

That you may leave
to me.

CHRYSOTHEMIS

But even if a knife—

ELECTRA

contemptuously

A knife!

CHRYSOTHEMIS

Or else an axe—

ELECTRA

An axe!
The axe! the axe with which our father—

CHRYSOTHEMIS

You?

O, horrid, you have it?

ELECTRA

I kept it
for our brother. Now we must swing it.

CHRYSOTHEMIS

You? these arms to slay Aegisthus?

ELECTRA

First him, then her; first her, then him, no matter.

CHRYSOTHEMIS

I am afraid. You are beside yourself.

ELECTRA

No one sleeps in their anteroom.

CHRYSOTHEMIS

Murder them in their sleep, and then live on!

ELECTRA

My concern is with him, and not with us.

CHRYSOTHEMIS

If only you came to your senses to see this madness!

ELECTRA

One who sleeps is a fettered victim. Did they
not sleep together, I could accomplish it
alone. But so, you must go along.

CHRYSOTHEMIS

warding her off

Electra!

ELECTRA

You! for you are strong!

Close to her

How strong you are!
the virgin nights have made you strong.
Your hips, how slender and lithe they are!
You can twist yourself through every crevice,
pull yourself through a window! Let me feel
your arms: how cool and strong they are!
As you struggle against me, I feel what arms
they are. You could crush whatever you clasp
in your arms. You could press me, or a man,
against your cool firm breasts with your arms
and one would suffocate! Everywhere
there is such strength in you! It flows like cool
pent-up water from the rock. It streams down
with your hair upon your strong shoulders!

CHRYSOTHEMIS

Let me go!

ELECTRA

No: I will hold on to you!
With my wretched withered arms I will
embrace your body, the more you struggle
the firmer you tie the knot, and I will wind
myself around you, sink my roots
deep into you and implant my will
into your blood!

CHRYSOTHEMIS

Let me go!

Flees a few steps.

ELECTRA

wildly after her, seizes her by her robe

No!

CHRYSOTHEMIS

Electra!

Let me go!

ELECTRA

I will not let you go.
We must grow so close together that the knife
which would tear my body from yours would kill
us both at once, for now we are alone
in this world.

CHRYSOTHEMIS

Electra, listen to me.
You are so clever, help us to get away
from this house, set us free.

Electra

without hearing her
You are full of strength,
your sinews are the sinews of a colt,
slender are your feet, easily I clasp them
with my arms as with a rope. I can feel
the warm blood through the coolness of your skin,
against my cheek I can feel the down
on your youthful arms: You are like fruit
on the day of its ripeness. From now on
I will be your sister as I have never
been your sister before! I will sit
in your chamber with you and will wait
for the bridegroom, I will anoint you
for him, and you shall dip yourself
in the fragrant bath like the young swan
and shelter your head at my breast
before he takes you, gleaming like a torch
through the veils, with his strong arms
into the wedding bed.

Chrysothemis

closes her eyes

No, sister, no.
Do not speak such words in this house.

Electra

Ah, yes! far more than a sister I will be
to you from this day on: I will serve you
like your slave. When you lie in travail,
I will stand at your bed by day and night,
keep off the flies, and draw the cool water,
and when all at once a living thing
lies in the naked lap, frightening almost,

then I will lift it up for you, so high!
that his smile may fall from on high
into the deepest secret caverns
of your soul and the last icy horror
there may melt under this sun and you may
weep it out in heavy tears.

CHRYSOTHEMIS

Oh,
take me away! I die in this house!

ELECTRA

at her knees

Your mouth is beautiful when it opens
to speak in anger! A dreadful cry
must spurt from your clean strong mouth,
dreadful like the cry of the goddess
of death, when someone lies like this
beneath you as I do now: when one awakens
suddenly and finds you like the goddess
of death above one's head! when one lies
bound beneath you and so looks up at you,
forced to look up at your slender body
with staring eyes, as ship-wrecked sailors
look up at the cliff before they die.

CHRYSOTHEMIS

What are you saying?

ELECTRA

rising

Before you escape
from this house and me, you must do it!

Chrysothemis wants to speak.

ELECTRA

covers her mouth with her hand

There is
no way out but this. I will not let you
go before you have sworn mouth to mouth
that you will do it.

CHRYSOTHEMIS

wrenches herself free

Let me go!

ELECTRA

seizes her again

Swear
that you will come tonight, when all is still,
to the foot of the stairs.

CHRYSOTHEMIS

Let me go!

ELECTRA

holds her by her robe

Child, do not resist!
Not one drop of blood will cling to your body;
quickly you shall slip out of the bloodstained robe
and with a clean body into the wedding shirt.

CHRYSOTHEMIS

Let me go!

ELECTRA

Do not be cowardly! The shuddering
fear which now you overcome will be repaid
with shudders of bliss night after night—

CHRYSOTHEMIS

I cannot!

ELECTRA

Say that you will come!

CHRYSOTHEMIS

I cannot!

ELECTRA

Look,
I lie before you, I am kissing your feet!

CHRYSOTHEMIS

escaping into the door of the house

I cannot!

ELECTRA

after her

A curse on you!

To herself, with savage resolution

Well then alone!

She begins digging eagerly near the wall of the house, to the side of the doorsill, without making a sound, like an animal. She pauses, looks around, digs again.

Orestes stands in the courtyard door, his figure set off in black against the last gleam of light. He enters. Electra looks at him. He turns slowly around so that his glance falls on her. Electra starts up violently; she trembles.

ELECTRA

What do you want, stranger? Why do you prowl
here at this dark hour, spying out
what others do! Maybe you have yourself

something in your mind that you would not want
others to discover. Then leave me to myself.
There is one thing I must do here. What is it to you!
Begone and let me burrow in the earth.
Do you hear when you are spoken to? or does
your curiosity not let you go? I do not
bury anything, I am digging something up.
And not the dead bone of a little child
which I covered days ago. No, my fellow,
I gave no life, and so I need not smother
a life nor bury it. When the earth's body
will some day take something from my hands,
it will be what I came out of, not what came
out of me. I am digging something up:
as soon as you stand back from the light, I'll
have it and caress it and I'll kiss it as if it were
my dear brother and my dear son, all in one.

ORESTES

Have you then nothing on earth that is dear to you
since you want to scrape a thing out of the earth
and kiss it? Are you all alone?

ELECTRA

I am no mother, I have no mother,
I am no sister, I have no sister,
I lie before the door yet I am not
the watchdog, I speak and yet I do not answer,
live and do not live, have long hair and yet
feel nothing of what, they say, all women feel:
in short, I beg you, go and leave me! leave me! leave me!

ORESTES

I must wait here.

ELECTRA

Wait here?

A pause

ORESTES

But you belong here
to this house? you are one of the maidservants
of the house?

ELECTRA

Yes, I serve here in this house.
But you have no cause to meddle here. Be glad
and go.

ORESTES

I told you that I must wait here
until they call me.

ELECTRA

They, in there? You lie.
I know well enough the master is not home.
And she, what should she want with you?

ORESTES

I and one
who is with me, we have a message to bring
to the mistress.

Electra is silent.

ORESTES

We have been sent to her
because we can bear witness that her son
Orestes died before our eyes.
For he was killed by his own horses.
I was as old as he and his companion
by day and night; the other one
who is with me, an old man, he was
our guardian and tutor.

ELECTRA

Did I yet have to
look upon you! did you have to crawl
down here into my wretched corner,
herald of misery! Can you not trumpet
forth your message where it gives pleasure!
You live—and he, who was better than you
and nobler a thousand times, and a thousand times
as important that he should live—he is dead!
Your eye stares at me and his is jellied.
Your mouth opens and shuts and his is
crammed full of earth. Oh, that I could cram
yours with curses! Get out of my sight.

ORESTES

But what do you want with me? they receive it
with pleasure here in the house. Let the dead be dead.
Let Orestes be. Well now, Orestes
has died, and it all had to come
as it did come. He rejoiced too much
in his life, and the gods up there
cannot endure the ringing sound of joy,
they detest the vigorous beat of wings
before evening, quickly they reach
for an arrow and nail the living creature
to the dark tree of his hidden fate
which had long since somewhere secretly
grown for him. And so he had to die.

ELECTRA

How he speaks of dying, this young fellow!
As if he had tasted it and spewed it out
again. But I! But I! to lie here knowing
that the child will never come again,
that they in there are alive and rejoice,

that this brood lives in its cave and eats
and drinks and sleeps and multiplies
while the child lingers down below
in the pit of horror and does not dare
come near his father. And I up here,
alone! living a lonely and horrible life
unlike even the beast in the forest.

ORESTES

But then,
who are you?

ELECTRA

What do you care who I am.
Did I ask you who you were?

ORESTES

I cannot help thinking:
You must be related by blood to those
who died, Agamemnon and Orestes.

ELECTRA

Related? I am this blood! I am the brutishly
spilled blood of King Agamemnon!
Electra is my name.

ORESTES

No!

ELECTRA

He denies it.
He scoffs at me and takes my name from me.
Since I have no father and no brother
I am the laughingstock of boys! Whoever
comes along the way kicks me with his foot,
they leave me not even my name!

ORESTES

Electra must be
ten years younger than you. Electra is tall,
her eye is sad but gentle whereas yours
is full of blood and hatred. Electra dwells
apart from men, and her day is spent
with tending a grave. Two or three women
she has about her who serve her silently.
And animals steal timidly around her dwelling
and nestle against her robe when she goes by.

ELECTRA

claps her hands

Good! Good! Tell me more fine things
about Electra. I'll repeat them to her

with a choking voice

when I see her.

ORESTES

Then I see her? I really
see her? You?

quickly

So they let you starve or—
have they been beating you?

ELECTRA

Who are you
that you ask so many questions?

ORESTES

Tell me!
Tell me! Speak!

ELECTRA

Both! both! both! Queens
do not prosper when they are fed with the refuse
of the table's trimmings, priestesses
are not made for leaping under the whip
and in such brief rags instead of flowing
garments. Leave my dress alone, do not
burrow in it with your eyes.

ORESTES

Electra!
What have they done with your nights!
Your eyes are frightful.

ELECTRA

sullenly

Go into the house,
I have a sister there who keeps herself
for joyous feasts!

ORESTES

Electra, hear me.

ELECTRA

I do not want to know who you are, you shall not
come any closer to me. I want to see no one!

Crouches down, her face towards the wall.

ORESTES

Listen, I have no time. Listen. I may not
speak loudly. Listen to me: Orestes lives.

Electra spins around.

ORESTES

Make no sound. If you stir, you will
betray him.

ELECTRA

Then he is free? where is he?
Do you know, where? is he hiding? he lies
imprisoned! Crouching somewhere in a corner,
he is waiting for his death! I have to
see him die, they have sent you in order
to torture me, to pull my soul high up
with a rope and dash it down again
onto the ground!

ORESTES

He is uninjured
as I.

ELECTRA

Then save him! before they put him
to death. Can you not give him a sign?
I kiss your feet that you may give him
a sign. By your father's dead body
I entreat you to run as quickly as you can
and bring him away! The child must die
if he spends the night in this house.

ORESTES

By my father's dead body! The child came
to this house in order that still
this night they die who must die—

ELECTRA

struck by his tone

Who
are you?

*The dour Old Servant rushes in from the yard with-
out a sound, throws himself down before Orestes, kisses his
feet, rises quickly, looking around him fearfully, and rushes
out again without making a sound.*

ELECTRA

hardly controlling herself

Who are you? I am afraid.

ORESTES

gently

The dogs in the yard recognize me,
and my sister does not?

ELECTRA

cries out

Orestes!

ORESTES

feverishly

If anyone in the house has heard you, he has
now my life in his hand.

ELECTRA

very softly, tremulous

Orestes!
No one is stirring. O let me see
your eyes! No, you shall not touch me!
Move away, I feel ashamed before you.
I do not know how you can look at me.

I am no more than the corpse of your sister,
my poor child. I know I make you shudder
with dread. And yet I was a king's daughter!
I think I was beautiful: when I blew out
the lamp in front of my mirror, I felt
with chaste wonder how my naked body
gleamed immaculate through the sultry night
like something divine. I felt how the thin beam
of the moon bathed in its white nakedness
as in a pond, and my hair was such hair
as makes men tremble; this hair is wiry, soiled,
dishonored now! Do you understand that, brother!
These sweet feelings of wonder and awe I have
had to sacrifice to my father. When I
rejoiced in my own body, do you think
his sighs did not reach, his groans did not press
up to my bed? Jealous are the dead:
and he sent me hatred, hollow-eyed hatred
for my bridegroom. And I had to let the monster,
who breathes like a viper, come over me
into my sleepless bed, who forced me to know
all that goes on between man and woman. Alas,
the nights, those nights in which I understood!
My body was cold as ice and yet was charred,
consumed with fire inwardly. And when
at last I knew it all, then I was wise,
and the murderers—I mean mother and him
who is with her—could not endure
a single glance of mine!
Why do you look about so fearfully? Speak!
Speak to me! Why, your whole body shivers!

ORESTES

Let this body shiver. Do you think it would
not shiver far worse if it could guess
on what errand I shall be taking it?

ELECTRA

You are going to do it? Alone? You poor child.
Did you bring no friends with you?

ORESTES

Let it pass,
do not speak of it. My old tutor is
with me. But I am the one who will do it.

ELECTRA

I have never seen the gods, yet I know
they will be there with you to help you.

ORESTES

I do not know what the gods are like. I only
know they have imposed this deed on me,
and they will condemn me if I shrink back.

ELECTRA

You will do it!

ORESTES

Yes, yes. If only I did not
have to look first in my mother's eyes.

ELECTRA

Then look at me, what she has made of me.

Orestes looks at her sadly.

ELECTRA

O child! child! you come, stealthily
you have come, you speak of yourself
as of a dead man, and you are alive!

ORESTES

softly

Be careful!

ELECTRA

Who am I then that you cast
such loving glances at me? Look, I am
nothing at all. All that I was I have
had to surrender. Even my shame which is
sweeter than all, which like the milky
silvery haze around the moon envelops
every woman and which turns infamy away
from her and her soul! I have sacrificed
my shame, as if I had fallen into the hands
of bandits who have torn from my body
even the last garment! I am not
without my wedding night as the virgins are,
I have felt the agony of childbirth
and have brought nothing into the world,
and always I have been a prophetess
and have called forth nothing from me
and my body except curses and despair.
At night I did not sleep, I made my bed
in the tower, and I cried out in the yard
and whined with the dogs. I made myself hated
and I saw everything, everything
I have had to see like the watchman on top
of the tower, and day turned into night,
and night turned into day again, and I found
no delight in the sun and in the stars,
for everything was as nothing to me
for his sake, everything was but a token
to me, and every day was but a landmark
on the way!

ORESTES

O my sister.

ELECTRA

What is it?

ORESTES

Sister, does not our mother
resemble you?

ELECTRA

savagely

Resemble me? No.
I do not want you to look her in the face.
When she is dead, then let us look together
at her face. Brother, she threw a white shirt
over our father's head, and then she struck
at the thing which stood before her, which was
helpless, which had no eyes and could not turn
its face towards her, which could not set
its arms free—do you hear me?—at this
she struck from above with the axe raised high.

ORESTES

Electra!

ELECTRA

Her face is the face
of her deeds.

ORESTES

I will do it,
I will do it quickly.

ELECTRA

Blessed is he
who may do a deed! The deed is like
a bed on which the soul may rest,
like a bed of balsam, to rest the soul
which is a wound, a blight, an ulcer,
and a flame!

*Orestes' tutor stands in the courtyard door, a vigorous
old man with flashing eyes.*

ELECTRA

Brother, who is this man?

THE TUTOR

hurrying towards them

Are you out of your wits that you do not restrain
your tongue where one breath, one sound, a mere nothing
may destroy us and our work—

ELECTRA

Who is that?

ORESTES

Do you not know him? If you love me, thank him.
Thank him that I exist. This is Electra.

ELECTRA

You! you! oh, now it all is real! it all
ties together! Let me kiss your hands!
I know nothing of the gods, I do not know
what they are like, therefore I had rather
kiss your hands.

The Tutor

Hush, Electra, hush!

Electra

No, I want to shout with joy over you
because you have steered him to this place.
When I was full of hate, I kept my silence
amply. Hatred is nothing, it eats and eats
and consumes itself, and love is still less
than hatred, it reaches after everything
and cannot grasp anything, its hands
are like flames which grasp nothing, all thinking
is nothing, and what issues from the mouth
is a powerless breeze, only he is blessed
who is coming to do his deed! And blessed
who may touch him and who digs up the axe
for him out of the earth and who holds the torch
for him and who opens the door for him, blessed
is he who may listen at the door.

The Tutor

seizes her roughly and presses his hand over her mouth

Be silent!

To Orestes in great haste

She is waiting inside. Her maids are looking
for you. There is no man in the house. Orestes!

Orestes draws himself up, overcoming his horror.

*The door of the house lights up, and a servant appears
with a torch, behind her the Confidante. Electra has leaped
to the rear; she stands in the dark. The Confidante bows
down in the direction of the two strangers, beckons to them*

to follow her inside. The servant fastens the torch to an iron ring in the door-jamb. Orestes and the Tutor go in. Orestes closes his eyes for a moment, feeling giddy; the Tutor is close behind him; they exchange a quick glance. The door closes behind them.

ELECTRA

alone, in terrible suspense. She runs to and fro in a single straight line in front of the door, with lowered head, like the captive animal in its cage. Suddenly she stands still and says

I could not give him the axe!
They have gone, and I could not
give him the axe. There are no gods
in heaven!

Again a terrible moment of waiting. Then from inside the piercing cry of Clytemnestra.

ELECTRA

cries out like a demon

Once more, strike!

From inside a second cry.

From the living quarters, on the left, come Chryso-themis and a swarm of servants.

Electra stands at the door, with her back pressed against the door.

CHRYSOTHEMIS

Something must have happened.

ONE OF THE SERVANTS

She cries out
like that in her sleep.

SECOND SERVANT

There must be men inside.
I heard men's footsteps.

THIRD SERVANT

All the doors
are bolted.

FOURTH SERVANT

They are murderers!
There are murderers in the house!

FIRST SERVANT

cries out

Oh!

ALL OF THEM

What is it?

FIRST SERVANT

Don't you see, there at the door
stands one!

CHRYSOTHEMIS

It is Electra! why, that is Electra!

SECOND SERVANT

Then why does she not speak?

CHRYSOTHEMIS

Electra,
Why do you not speak?

FIRST SERVANT

I will go out
and bring the menfolk.

Runs out, right.

CHRYSOTHEMIS

Why don't you open the door
for us, Electra!

SEVERAL

Electra, let us into the house!

FIRST SERVANT

coming back through the courtyard door, crying

Get back!

All are terrified.

FIRST SERVANT

Aegisthus! Back to our quarters! quick!
Aegisthus is coming through the yard! If he should
find us and something has happened in the house,
he will have us killed.

ALL OF THEM

Quick, back! quick inside!

They disappear into the house, left.

AEGISTHUS

at the entrance on the right

Is no one here to light my way? Will not one
of these villains stir? Can this race never
be taught discipline!

Electra takes the torch from its ring, runs down the steps to meet him, bows before him.

Aegisthus

is frightened of this dishevelled figure in the flickering light; he retreats before her.

Who is this sinister woman?
I have forbidden that an unknown face
come near me!

Recognizes her, angrily

What, is it you?
Who bids you come to meet me?

Electra

May I

not light your way?

Aegisthus

Well now, this news
concerns you above all. Where can I find
the strangers who bring this message to us
about Orestes?

Electra

Inside. They found
a kind hostess, and they amuse themselves
with her.

Aegisthus

And they truly report that he
is dead, and bring such reports that there can be
no doubt?

ELECTRA

O my lord, they report it not merely
with words, no, but with actual tokens
which cannot possibly be doubted.

AEGISTHUS

What is that in your voice? And what
has come over you that you fawn
on me so? Why do you stagger
back and forth with your light!

ELECTRA

It is only
that I learned good sense at last and stick
to those who are the stronger. Will you
permit me to go before and light your way?

AEGISTHUS

Up to the door. What are you dancing for?
Watch the way.

ELECTRA

*as she circles around him in a kind of weird dance, sud-
denly bowing very low*

Here! the steps,
lest you fall.

AEGISTHUS

at the house door

Why is there no light here?
Who are they over there?

ELECTRA

They are the men
who want to wait upon you in person, my lord.
And I who often annoyed you with my bold
immodest presence, now I will learn
at last to withdraw at the right moment.

AEGISTHUS

*goes into the house. A short silence. Then noise inside.
Immediately Aegisthus appears at the small window on the
right, rips away the curtain, cries*

Help! murder! help your master! murder! murder!
They are murdering me!

He is dragged away.

Does no one hear me?
does no one hear?

Again his face appears at the window.

ELECTRA

stretches to her full height

Agamemnon hears you!

AEGISTHUS

is being pulled away

Woe is me!

Electra stands facing the house, breathing furiously.

*The women come running out wildly, Chrysothemis
among them. As if out of their senses they rush towards the
courtyard door. There they suddenly stop, turn back.*

CHRYSOTHEMIS

Electra! Sister! Come with us! do come
with us! Our brother is inside the house!
It is Orestes who has done it!

A confused din of voices, a commotion outside.

Come!
He is standing in the antehall, and all are
gathered round him, they kiss his feet,
all who hated Aegisthus in their hearts
have flung themselves against the others,
everywhere, in every courtyard, lie
the dead, all who live are spattered with blood
and have wounds themselves, and yet their faces
beam, they all embrace—

*Increasing noise outside, the women have run out,
Chrysothemis is alone, light is falling in from the outside.*

and shout for joy,
a thousand torches have been lit. Don't you hear;
well, can't you hear?

ELECTRA

crouching on the doorsill

Do I not hear? can I
not hear the music? why, it is coming
from inside me. The multitude who carry torches
and whose steps, whose endless myriad footsteps
make the earth resound with hollow rumbling
everywhere, they all are waiting for me:
I know very well that they are waiting for me,
because I must lead the dance, and I cannot;
the ocean, the enormous twentyfold ocean

buries my every limb with his weight, I cannot
raise myself!

CHRYSOTHEMIS

almost shouting from excitement

Don't you hear, they carry him,
they carry him on their hands, their faces
are quite changed, their eyes are glistening
and their old cheeks, with tears! They are
all weeping, can you not hear it? Ah!

She runs out.

Electra has risen. She comes striding down from the doorsill. She has thrown back her head like a maenad. She flings her knees up high, she stretches her arms out wide; it is a nameless dance in which she strides forward.

CHRYSOTHEMIS

reappears at the door, behind her torches, a crowd of people, faces of men and women

Electra!

ELECTRA

stops, looks at her fixedly

Be silent and dance. All must
approach! here join behind me! I bear the burden
of happiness, and I dance before you.
For him who is happy as we, it behooves him to do
only this: to be silent and dance!

She takes a few more steps of the tensest triumph and collapses.

CHRYSOTHEMIS

rushes to her. Electra lies rigid. Chrysothemis runs to the door of the house, pounds on it.

Orestes! Orestes!

Silence.

CURTAIN

The Tower

A Tragedy in Five Acts (New Version)

Characters

KING BASILIUS

SIGISMUND, *his son*

JULIAN, *Governor of the Tower*

ANTON, *his servant*

BROTHER IGNATIUS, *formerly the Grand Almoner, Cardinal and Chancellor of the Realm*

OLIVIER, *a soldier*

A PHYSICIAN

THE VAIVODE OF LUBLIN

THE PALATINE OF KRAKOW

THE LORD CHANCELLOR OF LITHUANIA

THE CHIEF CUPBEARER

COUNT ADAM, *a Chamberlain*

STAROSTA OF UTARKOW

THE KING'S CONFESSOR

SIMON, *a Jew*

A GROOM

AN OFFICER

A COUNTRYWOMAN

ARON, *the Tartar* ⎫
JERONIM, *a scribe* ⎬ *rebels*
INDRIK, *the Latvian* ⎭

GERVASY ⎫ *the King's spies*
PROTASY ⎭

Courtiers, chamberlains, pages, a man with a wooden leg, a castellan, soldiers, a gatekeeper, a beggar, monks, rebels.

143

ACT I, Scene 1

(*In front of the tower. Outworks, partly built of stone, partly hewn into the rock. Between the enclosing walls growing dusk while the sky is still light. Olivier, the lance-corporal, and a few invalid soldiers, among them Aron, Pankraz, and Andreas, stand in a group.*)

OLIVIER. (*calls to the rear*) Recruit! Come here!

RECRUIT. (*A young country lad with flaxen hair rushes up.*)

OLIVIER. Run, fellow, and bring me fire for the pipe!

RECRUIT. Yessir. (*Wants to go.*)

ARON. Very good, sir, my corporal! That's how you say it!

OLIVIER. Get me the fire! Off with you!

RECRUIT. Yessir.

(*After a pause.*)

ANDREAS. Is it true, corporal, that you used to be a scholar?

OLIVIER. (*does not reply. Pause.*)

PANKRAZ. So you are our new corporal of the guard?

OLIVIER. (*does not reply.*)

RECRUIT. (*brings a glowing torch.*)

OLIVIER. Which way's the wind?

RECRUIT. Don't know, sir.

OLIVIER. Stand beween the pipe and the wind, you dumb beast.

RECRUIT. Yessir.

OLIVIER. (*lights his pipe*) This damned rapping noise must stop. Get going Aron. This is an order. No woodchopping around here. It bothers me.

PANKRAZ. Nobody's chopping wood. It's him back there: the prisoner.

OLIVIER. The prince who goes naked, with an old wolf's hide round his body?

PANKRAZ. (*looks around*) You must say: the prisoner. Don't let that other word slip out of your mouth. Or else you'll be up before the provost.

OLIVIER. (*laughs noiselessly.*)

ARON. Not in these times, they can't push a man like him around.

OLIVIER. (*looks toward the left*) What is the beast up to? Why does he make such a row in his cage?

ARON. He has scraped up a horse bone; he knocks about with it among the rats and the toads, like a madman.

PANKRAZ. They torment him, and so he torments them.

RECRUIT. He has a wolf's body, and out of it has grown a human head. He stretches out five-fingered hands and folds 'em like a man.

OLIVIER. Does it look that rare, the creature? Then I must see him. Recruit, throw a rock and rouse him.

(*He takes a pike and approaches.*)

ARON. He cannot hold up under his eyes! Look, how he crawls away, the wolfman.

ANDREAS. (*steps close to Olivier*) I warn you, corporal. Think of the strict instructions.

OLIVIER. Don't know of any.

ANDREAS. There are ten forbidden points—on those everybody here must take his oath.

ARON. He hoots at those! what, Olivier?

ANDREAS. Not less than ten paces from the prisoner. Not a word to him, not a word about him, on your body and your life.

PANKRAZ. Those the governor issued, and we are all subject to his sovereign rule.

ANDREAS. He has summary rights. He has power over our necks.

ARON. Power! Over thieves and beggars maybe, over such

145

sickly freebooters as you are! Not over a person like this one here!

OLIVIER. Where is the governor? I want to see him!

PANKRAZ. You won't see *him*. When he has an order to give, the bugle calls to attention three times. Then he sends his servant.

ARON. His snotty lackey to this martial personage? Did you hear that?

OLIVIER. Hold your brutish tongue, till the time comes.— Listen, there! The bagpipes. Now they sound again. And now, silent. Signals, that's what it is. Jews, smugglers.

ARON. We ought to scout them.

OLIVIER. Let them be. Comes in handy, the things they smuggle in.

ARON. What is it?

OLIVIER. (*in a low voice*) Arms, powder and shot, pikes, cudgels, hatchets. Coming up from Hungary, over from Bohemia, down from Lithuania.

ARON. Accursed Jews!

OLIVIER. (*in an undertone*) They smell what's going on. Smell it beforehand, the fiery red cock on the roof.

ARON. (*close by him*) And are *they* all agreed on this, tell me, my valiant captain!

OLIVIER. You will find out when the time comes.

RECRUIT. (*secretly, fearfully*) A three-legged hare was seen, a lean pig came down the road, a calf with glowing eyes runs through the streets.

OLIVIER. (*to Aron alone*) All against all. Not a house will be left standing. And what's left of the churches they'll sweep up with brooms.

ARON. And what will become of those who are the masters today?

OLIVIER. They will tumble head over heels into the privy.

ARON. Ah, such words run warm through my belly like a dram of brandy. And there'll be so many of us that we will overpower them?

OLIVIER. (*in an undertone*) Ten thousand in the houses, ten thousand in the forests, a hundred thousand under ground.

THE ONE WITH THE WOODEN LEG. (*who up to now has been silent*) They will draw him out and take him up, and the lowest will come to be the highest, and this one will be the poor man's king and he will ride on a white horse.

ARON. Shut up, Moravian Brother.

THE ONE WITH THE WOODEN LEG. In the moist mountains a kingdom will be founded by him.

ARON. Hold your filthy tongue!

OLIVIER. (*low, to Aron*) Even such as he we shall need. And the one back there, also. That one I'll train like a dog; he shall jump and retrieve for me.

ARON. I do not understand it, but I know that you will be a commander. For you look upon men as one looks upon stones.

OLIVIER. He will command who has the political fatality on his side.

ARON. Is it so high and mighty, this fatality?

(*A horn signal. Another. And yet another.*)

PANKRAZ. (*softly*) There you are. He has them signal three times to attention. And here comes his footman.

ANTON. (*appears on a wooden bridge over the outworks and starts coming down.*)

(*The soldiers, except Olivier, move away.*)

ANTON. (*steps toward Olivier from behind*) Delivering an order—(*greeting.*)

OLIVIER. (*does not respond.*)

ANTON. By order of His Excellency!

(*Greets again behind Olivier's back.*)

OLIVIER. (*turns around, measures Anton with a contemptuous look.*)

ANTON. (*greets him again, very friendly*) Wishing the commander of the guard a good day.—By general order: He should withdraw his guard from here and occupy the entrances. But his posts must turn their backs and all the same keep their eyes open. Nothing that will take place down here is of any concern to the corporal and the guard—but I am going to tell you: the prisoner will be led out for medical inspection. You understand, sir? I beg you, sir, execute the order.

OLIVIER. (*spits and goes off.*)

ANTON. (*looking after him*) A free-spirited soldier-like young man. Standing here and talking with him for one moment is like discoursing for an hour with another.

OLIVIER. (*outside*) Mount guard! Right turn!

(Short roll of drums.)

PHYSICIAN. (*comes downstage the same way as Anton*) Where do I find the sick man?

ANTON. You mean to say, sir: the prisoner. Be patient, sir. I'll bring the creature out to you.

PHYSICIAN. Where is the chamber?

ANTON. What chamber?

PHYSICIAN. Well, the prison, the keep.

ANTON. (*points toward the back*) There!

PHYSICIAN. What, there? (*turns in the direction*) I see a small, open cage, not good enough for a dog kennel.—You do not mean to tell me that in there he—or else an offense has been committed here which cries up to heaven!

ANTON. (*shrugs his shoulders.*)

PHYSICIAN. In there? Day and night?

ANTON. Winter and summer. In the winter, a half load straw is thrown in.

PHYSICIAN. Since when? How long?

ANTON. Four years ago things became a bit worse. Since then he spends also the nights there in the cage, has no freedom to go about, his feet on the chain, with a heavy ball to it, the stinking hide 'round his body, summer and winter, sees the sun no more than two hours altogether and only in mid-summer. (*The dull sound of strokes is again audible as in the beginning.*)

PHYSICIAN. (*steps nearer*) My eye is getting accustomed. I see an animal which cowers on the ground.

(*Steps back.*)

ANTON. Aye, that is the one in question.

PHYSICIAN. That!—Call him. Lead him out here in front of me.

ANTON. (*looks around*) I must not speak with him in the presence of a stranger.

PHYSICIAN. I shall take the responsibility.

ANTON. Sigismund!—He doesn't answer.—Take care! He can't bear it if anybody comes near him. Once he locked teeth with a fox which the guards threw over the rail, for the sport of it.

PHYSICIAN. Can you not call to him? coax him? Is there no human reason in him?

ANTON. He? He knows Latin and runs through a stout book as if it were a flitch o' bacon.

(*Approaches the cage calling in softly*)

Come now, Sigismund. Why, who might it be? It's Anton himself is here.

(*He opens the gate with a pike which had been leaning against the wall.*)

There, now I put down my stick.

(*He places the pike on the ground.*)

Now I sit down on the ground. Now I sleep.

(*Softly to the physician*)

Take care, sir. He must not get frightened, or there'll be trouble.

PHYSICIAN. Why, has he a weapon?

ANTON. Always a horse bone. They must have once buried the carcass in the corner. —Deep inside, it is a good creature; if it please, sir, give him something that he may grow gentle again.

PHYSICIAN. When the whole world lies heavy upon him. All things somehow are bound up together.

ANTON. Ssst! he is moving. He is looking at the open gate. That is something unusual!

SIGISMUND. (*steps out of his cage, a large rock in one hand.*)

ANTON. (*beckons to him*) Come and sit down, next to me.

SIGISMUND. (*echoes the words*) Sit down next to me!

ANTON. (*sitting on the ground*) A gentleman has come.

SIGISMUND. (*notices the physician, shudders convulsively.*)

ANTON. Don't be afraid. A good gentleman. What will he think of you? Put the rock down. He thinks you are a child. And you, full twenty years old.

(*Stands up, goes slowly towards him, and gently wrests the rock out of his hand.*)

PHYSICIAN. (*without taking his eyes off Sigismund*) A monstrous offense. Unthinkable, this!

ANTON. Salute the gentleman! or what will he think? He has come from far away.

PHYSICIAN. (*steps nearer*) Would you like to live somewhere else, Sigismund?

SIGISMUND. (*looks up to him, then looks away; he speaks half to himself, rapidly like a child*)
Beasts are of many kinds, all rushing at me. I cry: Not too close! Wood-lice, worms, toads, goblins, vipers! all want to fall upon me. I beat them to death, it sets them free, come the tough black beetles, bury the lot.

PHYSICIAN. Bring me light, I must look into his eye.

ANTON. I can't leave you alone with him, sir; I am not allowed to do that!

(*Calls to the rear*) A torch there!

PHYSICIAN. (*goes toward Sigismund, places a hand on his forehead. Horn signal outside.*) What is that?

ANTON. It means that nobody must come near, they shoot to kill.

SIGISMUND. (*very rapidly*) Your hand is good, help me now! Where have they put me? Am I now in the world? Where is the world?

PHYSICIAN. (*to himself*) The whole world is just enough to fill our mind and heart when we look out at it through the small peephole from the safety of our house. But woe! when the dividing wall breaks down!

(*A soldier brings a burning pine-torch.*)

ANTON. Here is the torch! (*Hands it to the physician.*)

PHYSICIAN. I must see his eye.

(*Presses Sigismund, who leans against his knees, softly towards himself and illuminates his face from above.*)

God knows, it is not a murderous eye; only an unfathomable abyss. Soul and anguish without end.

(*He returns the torch; Anton stamps it out.*)

SIGISMUND. Light is good. Enters in, makes the blood clean. Stars are such light. Inside me is a star. My soul is holy.

PHYSICIAN. A ray of light must have once touched him which has awakened his innermost life. Then he has been doubly wronged.

(*Julian, the governor, accompanied by a soldier who carries a lantern, appears above on the wooden bridge and looks down.*)

ANTON. His Excellency himself is here. They signal up there, so the examination must come to an end.

151

PHYSICIAN. I determine that. (*He takes Sigismund's pulse*) What do you give him to eat?

ANTON. (*softly*) It's too mean for a mangy dog. Sir, if you could speak a word about this!

PHYSICIAN. I have finished.

ANTON. Now Sigismund goes in again.

(*Sigismund shudders, kneels on the ground. Anton takes up the pike, opens wide the gate into the cage. Sigismund remains on his knees, stretches out his hand.*)

PHYSICIAN. (*covers his eyes*) Oh human kind! Man! Man!

(*Sigismund expels a sound of lamentation.*)

ANTON. Shall they come with poles to drive you in?

PHYSICIAN. I beg of you, go for now to your place. I promise you that I shall do what I can.

(*Sigismund rises, bows toward the physician.*)

PHYSICIAN. (*to himself*) More than dignity in such abasement! This is a princely creature if ever one walked the earth.

(*Sigismund has returned to the cage.*)

ANTON. (*has shut the cage from the outside*) With your permission, sir, I'll go before you. Your honor is expected at once up in the tower.

(*They go up.*)

Scene 2

(*A room in the tower, a large and a smaller door. Julian, Anton.*)

JULIAN. Has Simon come in? He has been seen. As soon as he shows himself, report here.

ANTON. (*points behind him*) The doctor.

JULIAN. Let him enter.

(*Anton opens the small door. The physician enters, makes a bow. Anton leaves.*)

JULIAN. I am very obliged to you, sir, for your troublesome journey here.

PHYSICIAN. You were pleased to command, your Excellency.

JULIAN. (*after a short pause*) You have examined this person?

PHYSICIAN. With horror and astonishment.

JULIAN. How do you judge the case?

PHYSICIAN. As a dreadful crime.

JULIAN. I am asking for a medical report.

PHYSICIAN. The outcome will prove whether, among the rest, the physician has not been called too late.

JULIAN. I should hope not! Make use, sir, of your renowned abilities. No expense shall be shunned.

PHYSICIAN. Only quackery would attempt to heal the body through the body alone. More is at stake. The enormous crime has been perpetrated upon all mankind.

JULIAN. How do you, sir, arrive at such irrelevancies? Our concern is with a single private person who is in my keeping.

PHYSICIAN. Not at all. In the spot where this life is plucked out by its roots there rises a turbulence which carries us all along with it.

JULIAN. (*gazes at him*) You presume a good deal.—You are a famous person, doctor. The medical faculty is ill-disposed toward you, but that has only helped to make you more prominent. You have a great sense of your own worth.

PHYSICIAN. Your Excellency cannot possibly conceive how slight is my regard for myself. My renown is in many ways a misunderstanding. To those who walk in a mist even a torch looks grand like a church portal.

JULIAN. (*walks up and down, then suddenly stopping in front of the physician*) Speak out, straight from the heart! Who do you suspect is the prisoner? Answer without fear. I ask you as a private person.

PHYSICIAN. Whatever the capacity in which you ask me—I have only one and the same word for it: here is a being of the noblest order held in the most piteous degradation.— Your most noble person alone, who lend yourself to be keeper and jailer of an unknown—

JULIAN. Leave our self out of it. I see you have come here in a singularly prejudiced frame of mind.

PHYSICIAN. I judge by no reports, only by my impression. This living being before whom I stood down there, up to his ankles in filth, is a *quinta essentia* of the highest earthly virtues.

JULIAN. You are pleased to speak in fancy, without insight into circumstances. I remain with realities, insofar as the state secret does not shut my lips. The specimen of young manhood in question was a victim of coincidences. I have done what I could. Without me he would be hardly alive.

PHYSICIAN. He would be alive without you as without me, and when his hour comes, he will go forth. That is the sense of the coincidences.

(*A knock on the door.*)

JULIAN. (*looks at him*) I wish to converse with you further. Above all about what is to be done. The prisoner, I admit it, has been neglected. You will propose incisive measures to me.

(*Physician bows. Anton has entered, with cups on a silver tray.*)

JULIAN. For the moment I am prevented. In the adjoining room a light refreshment has been served for you.

(*Anton responding to a sign comes up with the cups.*)

JULIAN. (*takes one cup*) A stirrup cup, I entreat you. My thanks once more for the sacrifice of valuable time. I pledge you.

PHYSICIAN. (*after he has drunk*) But scarcely touching the lips.

JULIAN. It has lately deprived me of sleep. There must be a poison in this precious drink as well as a balm.

(*He turns to Anton; they talk privately.*)

PHYSICIAN. Al-cohol: the most precious substance. It appears inside the body twenty-four hours after death, at the same moment when the first breath of decomposition sets in. Out of corruption the virtue of restoration. That is *en-heiresin naturae.*

ANTON. (*reports in an undertone*) The baptized Simon has come, with a letter for your Lordship.

JULIAN. Bring him in, at once.

ANTON. He is right here.

(*Lets Simon enter at the larger door. The physician has bowed and left at the smaller door. Simon hands Julian a letter.*)

JULIAN. Received in what way?

SIMON. In the known manner through the known person. I was told moreover to make haste: a matter of importance for your Lordship.

(*Julian hastily breaks the letter open, signals Simon to retire. Simon leaves.*)

JULIAN. (*reads the letter*)—The king's nephew killed during the hunt! Thrown into a wolf's pit with his horse!—It is uncanny. The young prince, twenty years of age, a robust youth. There is God's visible hand!

(*Walks up and down, and goes on reading*)

The king alone, for the first time alone, the first time in thirty years abandoned by his all-powerful adviser.

(*Reads*)

The cardinal-minister, your potent unyielding enemy, into the monastery, without the king's farewell—he has withdrawn his hand from the public affairs, for ever—

(*speaks*)

I am dreaming! it cannot possibly be that so much stands written on this small scrap of paper!

(*Steps to the window into the light, reads again*)

—fallen into a wolf's pit—the cardinal-minister into a monastery—divested himself of all temporal honors—under the name: Brother Ignatius—

(*He rings the hand bell. Simon enters.*)

JULIAN. I have here surprising reports. Great things have happened. —What is new in the world. What do people say?

SIMON. The world, most gracious Burgrave Excellency, the world is one big misery. When it's come to this, that you cannot buy anything with money—can you, with such money? What is money? Money is confidence in the full weight. And where can you find a silver taler? To see a solid coin these days, you have to go on a long journey.

JULIAN. (*to Anton*) The key!

ANTON. Excellency is holding it in your hand.—

JULIAN. The other one.

ANTON. Here it is, before your eyes.

SIMON. The war began; they paid the soldier, they paid the provisioner with silver talers. The war goes into the second year, and the taler becomes a mixture. In the third year the silver was silver-plated copper. But they took it, people took it. The king finds out he can coin money by printing his face and his arms on tin, on lead, on muck. So the great lords saw it can be done, and the burghers, and the gentry, too. If the king coins money, the lords coin money; who does not coin money? Until everything swims in money.

(*Julian has fixed his eyes again upon the letter.*)

SIMON. However, if you have paid out solid coin, should you take back light-weight money? But how can you not take it? Since the king's own

(*he removes his cap*)

sovereign likeness is stamped on it. But for tribute and tax the new money is prohibited! And the soldiers and the miners should take the light coin? So, what is happening? The miners don't go into the mines any more, the bakers don't bake bread any more, the doctor runs away from the sickbed, the student from the school, the soldier from the standard. And the king, his reliability is gone. Then there is in all the world nothing left to trust.

(*Noticing Julian's look*)

But what do I need to tell your gracious Excellency of all this? When this evening one of the very great lords from the court will ride in on horseback, he will talk over with your gracious Excellency the state affairs and the political—

JULIAN. (*startled*) Who will come riding here on horseback? What is that you are saying?

SIMON. The great Lord Vaivode of Lublin, with a following of at least fifty, among them noble pages and royal bodyguards, whom I have left behind by two, three hours.— Your gracious Excellency looks at me as if my mouth brought you a message of surprise where your Lordship is holding in your hands the letters in which it must be written down, black on white.

JULIAN. That is all. Let him go.

(*Simon leaves. Anton comes back in.*)

JULIAN. Anton! The proudest greatest Vaivode in the whole
court! Sent here, to me! From the king himself, sent to me!
Anton! they are bringing the corpse back to life! It is to
me—me—do you hear? What sort of faces are you pulling?

ANTON. As if I couldn't guess what is going on inside you!
This means, after all, no more and no less than this: they
are coming to bring you back to court, they are going to
press on you the honors, which means—the troubles, the
dignities, which means—the burdens, the trusted offices,
the sinecures and vexations, all the business you loathe as
the child does bitter medicine!

JULIAN. It cannot be true. —Oh God, if it were true!

ANTON. O you my Savior! How do we make our escape now!
How do we dodge this? Now good counsel is dear. If your
Lordship were to pretend sickness? I am going to make
the bed ready!

JULIAN. Stop that nonsense! The panelled room is to be furnished for his Highness the Vaivode. My own bed goes in.
My riding coat, have the marten-furs ripped out, make a
footrug out of them for his Grace, right beside his bed.

ANTON. In God's name, if only he set his foot somewhere else
soon enough!

JULIAN. Send the trumpeter up on the outworks!

ANTON. The trumpeter?

JULIAN. The moment he sees the cavalcade, one trumpet signal! One! make certain of this: if they are ordinary riders.
But if it is a princely cavalcade—

(*He must govern his excitement by holding on to the table.*)

ANTON. Then?

JULIAN. Then three flourishes in succession, as is done for
the king! —Why are you gaping at me? Shall I—

ANTON. I am not going to say a word.

(*Looks at him sideways*)

Must be a glorious feeling, when one knows: I am sure of myself! Come here, Satan, spread it out before me, the splendor, like a carpet—and now take it off quick before I spit on it because such things I have mastered in myself.

(*A knock on the door. Anton answers it.*)

The doctor has finished eating and begs permission to wait on you. —Shall he?
JULIAN. Let him enter. And then off with you to attend to my orders.

(*The physician has come in; he has a sheet of paper in his hand. Anton leaves.*)

PHYSICIAN. (*stopping before Julian who stands there lost in thought*) I find your Excellency much altered.
JULIAN. You are a keen physiognomist. —What is it you see in my features?
PHYSICIAN. A violent hopeful agitation. Far-reaching arrangements! Great preparations! Encompassing a whole empire. Your lordship is created of heroic stuff.

(*Julian is obliged to smile, but immediately suppresses his smile.*)

However—I must pronounce it in the same breath: the source itself is troubled, the deepest root is cankered. In this your imperious countenance Good and Evil wage a fearful coiling battle like serpents.
JULIAN. Give my pulse greater steadiness, that is all I need. I am about to face great excitement. —I need different nights.

(*Closes his eyes, quickly opens them again.*)

PHYSICIAN. (*fixing his eyes upon him*) Your pulse is not steady, and yet—I can answer for it—the heart muscle is powerful. But you deny your heart. —Heart and head must be one. But you have consented to the satanic split; you have suppressed the noble inner organ. Hence these bitterly curling lips, these hands which forbid themselves the touch of wife and child.

JULIAN. (*nods*) My years have been terribly lonely.

PHYSICIAN. Terrible, but so willed. What you are seeking is a keener desire: sovereignty, absolute power of command.

JULIAN. (*looks at him.*)

PHYSICIAN. I see heroic ambition in your carriage and gait, checked in the hips by an impotent will, gigantically warring with itself. Your nights are raging desire, powerless aspiration. Your days are boredom, self-consuming, doubting what is most high—the soul's wings shackled in chains!

JULIAN. You come close to one's self! Too close!

PHYSICIAN. To point to a malady where I see it, that is my part. The wrong done to this youth, the enormity of the crime, the complicity, the partial consent: all this stands written in your face.

JULIAN. Enough. You talk, sir, without knowledge of the matter.

(*Goes to the wall, causes a panel to fly open, takes out a sheet of paper from which hangs a seal.*)

I have saved his life, more than once. He was to vanish altogether, to be done away with. I was distrusted. I had handed him over to a good-hearted peasant family, from his eighth to his thirteenth year of life. And I was charged with having ambitious plans in connection with the prisoner's survival. I had to place him again inside the tower.

PHYSICIAN. I understand.

JULIAN. At first I had him kept in a humanly decent prison.— In the first night a shot was fired through the window and grazed his neck, a second one towards morning which went between his arm and his chest. —Without me he would have been murdered. —I wish not to be misjudged by you.

(*He holds the paper out to him.*)

You see, sir! The very highest seal. In his own handwriting the signature of the most exalted person in the realm. —I go very far with you.

PHYSICIAN. (*reads from the paper*) "convicted of a planned attempt on the life of his Sacred Majesty—" —That boy! —This writing is nine years old. At that time he was a child!

JULIAN. The stars had pointed to him before he was born as if with a blood-stained finger. What had been predicted was fulfilled, point by point, horribly to confirm him as the one who stands outside the human community. He was convicted before his lips could form a word.

PHYSICIAN. (*raises his hands to heaven*) Convicted!

JULIAN. Of high treason. —What is there in my power to do!

(*Locks the sheet away.*)

PHYSICIAN. (*takes a scrap of paper from his belt*) I wrote down while eating what I hold to be most indispensable. A place of custody worthy of human dignity, facing the sun, pure nourishment, the consolation of a priest.

JULIAN. Give it to me.

PHYSICIAN. No, it is too little; I shall tear it up. (*He does so.*) Only rebirth heals such a shattered life. Let him be brought back into his father's house, not a year from now, nor a month, but tomorrow at night!

JULIAN. (*up and down*) And if it is a demon and a devil, presumptuous man? A rebel against God and the world! — There!

(*He listens. Trumpets in the distance.*)

JULIAN. (*growing pale, closes his eyes*) You are accustomed to auscultation, sir; your ear is sharp. May I ask whether I hear rightly?

PHYSICIAN. Three trumpet flourishes at a great distance.

(*Julian opens his eyes again, draws a deep breath.*)

PHYSICIAN. At this instant you have given birth to a bold and frightful design. Your face is flaring up.

JULIAN. I see as through a sudden light the possibility of a trial.

PHYSICIAN. Whereby the unfortunate creature could be saved?

JULIAN. I hold it possible that much will be placed in my hands. Sir, as to a sure and effective, powerful sleeping-draught, are you capable—?

PHYSICIAN. May I ask—

JULIAN. I would send out a rider for it.

PHYSICIAN. Do I guess correctly? You wish to transport the unconscious body to another place. Bring certain persons before his eyes?

JULIAN. We will not speak one word too much. I am risking my head.

PHYSICIAN. And if he fails the test? —If he dissatisfies. —What becomes of him?

JULIAN. Then it may—perhaps—be possible to spare him and protract the same life which he has led till now.

PHYSICIAN. I will not be an accomplice in this.

(*Steps back*)

It would mean driving one of God's creatures into madness.

JULIAN. I give you half a minute's time to reflect. Consider it.

PHYSICIAN. (*after a few seconds*) Your rider can get the draught from me tomorrow night. —The dose is strictly measured out. Your Excellency bind yourself solemnly to me that from no other hand shall the prisoner—

JULIAN. From my own hand. Provided that I can effect the trial. That rests with higher persons.

(*He trembles, rings the hand bell.*)

PHYSICIAN. I am discharged?

JULIAN. With the request that you accept this trifling pay-ment (*hands him a purse*) and in addition this ring as a memento. (*Draws the ring off his finger, holds it out; his hand trembles visibly.*)

PHYSICIAN. Your Lordship rewards nobly.

(*Makes a bow, and withdraws.*)
(*Anton enters by the other door, a rich mantle over his arm, and shoes in his hand. Hurriedly he helps Julian re-move the house robe and put on the rich coat.*)

JULIAN. How close are they? I saw a single rider gallop in.

ANTON. Yes, yes. (*Fastens the garment.*)

JULIAN. An outrider, a courier? What?

ANTON. I won't say it, it would annoy you. A puffed up groom!

JULIAN. What do they want of me?

ANTON. Just because the fellow brings a letter in the King's own hand, that goes right to his head, common lackey stable boy. Why shouldn't the King once in a while write a letter by himself? Has he no hands?

JULIAN. A hand-written letter—to me in person?

(*He has to sit down.*)

ANTON. (*helps put on his shoes*) Did I not know you would be annoyed? —But that it should touch you so to the quick—

(*Julian says nothing.*)

JULIAN. (*jumps up, out of breath*) Are the men posted?

ANTON. Lined up in formation.

(*Ties his shoes.*)

JULIAN. You, out front to the door, with a light.

ANTON. But the torches are up along the stairs. Who wants to tire himself out for people that only bring unwelcome trouble into the house!

JULIAN. A light! You are to kneel on the lowest landing. When his Grace, the Vaivode, has passed you, run ahead and light him up the stairs. I will come to meet him, three steps down from the upper landing, not a step further.

ANTON. (*lights a candlestick*) Just so. He shall understand, that court flunkey, that we haven't been waiting for him these nineteen years.

CURTAIN

ACT II, Scene 1

(*Cloisters. In the background, the entrance gate. On the right, the entrance into the monastery. The Father Superior, before him the two royal spies Gervasy and Protasy.*)

GERVASY. As we report, your Reverence. His exalted Highness in person, himself.

PROTASY. Yet wishes not to be known.

GERVASY. Known perhaps—but not recognized.

PROTASY. In strictest privacy, most extraordinary secrecy.

(*Knocking on the gate. The gatekeeper goes to open it.*)

GERVASY. With humble submission, we shall withdraw.

PROTASY. We will wait outside for his Grace, the Vaivode of Lublin. For he is summoned here.

(*They bow low and disappear in the cloisters. Father Superior leaves. The gatekeeper opens the gate. King Basilius and courtiers step in. A beggar enters behind them.*)

KING. Is this the place where Brother Ignatius receives those who come to him with a petition?

GATEKEEPER. Stand here all of you and wait.

YOUNG CHAMBERLAIN. Move on, you, and announce us as I shall tell you.

GATEKEEPER. I may not announce you. That is not my office. My office is to unlock the gate and to lock the gate.

YOUNG CHAMBERLAIN. Do you know in whose presence you are?

GATEKEEPER. I don't know, and I must not know. It is not my office. This one I know.

(*Points to the beggar, steps up to him.*)

Stand here. He will be joyful because you have come again.

(*The beggar stands silently to the side.*)

KING. This is a heavy errand. I will raise my cousins who have gone with me above all Vaivodes, Palatines, and Ordinants.

(*The courtiers bow.*)

YOUNG MONK. (*comes from the right; graceful, quiet, always smiling*) Speak softly!

KING. Is he asleep so early in the evening that he cannot be disturbed?

YOUNG MONK. Towards morning, when the stars become pale, only then does he fall asleep, and when the birds begin to stir, he is awake again.

(*Goes up to the beggar, who is praying, his face in his hands*)

What is your wish?

(*The beggar does not move.*)

GATEKEEPER. He is the one without a name who moves about the countryside from one holy place to the next and spends the nights, summer and winter, on stone church steps. He has once before spoken to him.

BEGGAR. (*removes his hand from his eyes; one of his eyes has been put out.*)
Unworthy!

GATEKEEPER. Marauding soldiers, such as you find everywhere nowadays, have struck out one of his eyes. But he has forgiven them and he prays for them.

BEGGAR. Unworthy!

(*Stands behind the courtiers.*)

KING. Announce us! Tell him there is someone here, Basilius, and in great need, and his petition is urgent.

YOUNG MONK. (*bows*) He will soon come. Be patient, gentlemen.

(*Goes in right; a muffled sound of singing voices becomes audible:* "Tu reliquisti me et extendam manum meam et interficiam te!")

KING. (*takes one step forward, looks upwards*) Today is St. Giles' Day: now the stag begins to be in rut. —A beautiful, bright evening: the magpies fly from their nest in pairs without fear for their young, and the fisherman is joyous: the fish will soon spawn, yet still they are eager and leap in the early mist of moonlight, ere night falls. For some time yet it remains light enough to find the mark between river and forest, and great and regal the stag steps out of the copse and parts his lips that it seems as if he laughed, and utters a mighty bell so that the animals in the underbrush press their shuddering flanks close one against the other, from terror and desire. —We were like him and we relished our days of majesty, before the weather turned, and the knees of beautiful women loosened at the sound of our coming, and where we chose to enter there the silver candelabra or the roseate torch illuminated the marriage of Jupiter with the nymph.

(*He supports himself on the young chamberlain.*)

And to all this no end seemed to be set, for our strength was royal. —But for a long time now hell has unleashed its powers against us; and there lurks a conspiracy against our fortune beneath our feet and above our hair, which bristles up, and we cannot grasp the rebels. We would go here and go there and strengthen our dominion, and it is as if the ground softened and our thighs sank into emptiness. The walls reel in their foundations, and our path has turned into an impassable bog.

ONE OF THE COURTIERS. The fault lies with the fattened burghers in the towns, these sausage-grinders and wool-carders and especially the Jews: they have sucked the country's marrow from the bones. They have drawn the silver out of the money and left in our hands stinking red copper, red as the hair on their heads, sons of Judas.

ANOTHER ONE. (*steps forward from the rear*) They lie bedded down on royal bonds as on goose feathers, their foxholes are papered with mortgage notes of counts and bannerets—and if you grasp ten thousand of them in your harnessed hands till they are crushed, then blood and sweat will flow unto the earth, and out of the ears of corn the gold and the silver will fall upon Polish ground.

THE FIRST ONE. Royal Majesty, let us ride out with our loyal vassals of noble blood against the Jews and their knaves that sit behind their palisades, against rebels, escaped monks, runaway school masters, and belabor them with as many swords, pikes, maces as have yet remained in our noble hands—before it is too late.

KING. I cannot seize the filthy rabble. I come riding up; they are beggars. Out of roofless hovels they come crawling towards me and stretch emaciated arms out to me. They feed on the barks of trees and stuff their bellies with clumps of earth.

(*He gazes before him; his head sinks thoughtfully on his breast.*)

This also was in the prophecy. There were horrors in it of which anyone would have said that they could be meant only as a likeness, and they begin to be fulfilled in the sense of the word itself. Starvation is in the prophecy; the plague is in the prophecy; darkness, illuminated by burning villages—the soldier who tears down the banner and with the halter strikes his commander in the face, the countryman who runs from his plough and hammers his scythe into the shape of a bloody pike—all these are in the prophecy.

(*He sighs deeply, forgetting those about him.*)

And then comes the chief part: that the rebellion gets its own banner: which is a bundle of clanking broken chains fixed to a blood-stained staff, and he before whom they carry it, he is my own son, —and his face is like a devil's face, and he does not sleep until he finds me and sets his foot upon my neck. —Thus was it prophesied! Word for word, written out, as I speak it!

(*He moans and recalls himself, looks back on his train of followers.*)

I feel very ill, my loyal men! I hope you have escorted me to a physician who can help me.

(*Brother Ignatius, the Grand Almoner, is led in from the right. Two monks support him. The young monk, seen before, walks by the side, an open book in his hand; a lay brother follows, carrying a folding chair. They place the chair and let the Grand Almoner sink down on it. He is ninety years old; his hands and face are yellowish white, like ivory. He keeps his eyes for the most part closed, but when he opens them, his look is still capable of spreading*) *fear and respect. He wears the habit of a simple monk. Everyone is silent from the moment he enters. The singing becomes distinctly audible, a single menacing voice:* "Ecce ego suscitabo super Babylonem quasi ventum pestilentem. Et mittam in Babyloniam ventilatores et ventilabunt eam et demolientur terram eius.")

GRAND ALMONER. (*with half-closed eyes*) The light of day. A fallow gloom. Read from Guevara. Here is a garden of flowers—gelatin, motley and stifling.

(*He closes his eyes.*)

CHOIR. "Et demolientur terram eius! Et cadent interfecti in terra Chaldaeorum."

GRAND ALMONER. (*opens his eyes, notices the beggar, beckons to him in a lively manner*)
Look now, what a guest has crossed our threshold!

(*The king relates this to himself, tries to step forward. The Grand Almoner, without regarding him, contemptuously waves his hand like one who drives off a fly.*)

COURTIERS. (*start up*) How! What! How dare he?

(*The king signals them to restrain themselves.*)

GRAND ALMONER. (*to the beggar, with eager interest*) How do you fare, my beloved? and will you now rest with us, at least one day and one night?

(*The beggar is silent.*)

GRAND ALMONER. Lead me to him if he will not come to me that I may embrace him and receive his blessing.

(*Attempts to rise, supported by the monks.*)

BEGGAR. Unworthy! (*Escapes.*)

CHOIR. "Et demolientur terram eius! Et cadent interfecti in terra Chaldaeorum."

GRAND ALMONER. Read out of Guevara, as long as the light lasts.

YOUNG MONK. (*raises the book and reads*) "World, depart from me, in your palaces they serve without payment, they caress in order to kill, they do honor in order to disgrace, they punish without forgiveness."

KING. (*approaches the Grand Almoner*) Cardinal, your king and master wishes you a good evening.

(*The Grand Almoner runs his hand through the air as if he were frightening off a fly.*)

COURTIERS. (*grumble among themselves, turn away as if they meant to leave*) Unheard of! Shameful spectacle!

KING. (*goes towards them*) Remain, my faithful! Do not go from me!

A COURTIER (*enraged, but with a subdued voice*) He should be dragged from his chair and his chops pressed in the ground!

KING. I will take from the royal townships their liberties! I will deny my protection to the Jews, and all shall be placed in your hands as it was wont to be in the time of our ancestors. Remain!

(*The courtiers bend their knees in reverence, kiss his hands and the hem of his garment. —The king smiles. The singing has stopped.*)

GRAND ALMONER. Read out of Guevara. I am weary that it is still day.

YOUNG MONK. (*reads*) "There the upright are pushed into the corner and the innocent convicted. There credit is given to them that lust after power and to the honest, none."—

KING. (*to the courtiers*) Leave us, all of you. Turn away. It must be done.

(*The courtiers go off and remain invisible. Also the monks, except one.*)

KING. (*approaches, falls on his knees in front of the Grand Almoner, and rises again.*)

GRAND ALMONER. (*looks at him, long and penetratingly*) I do not know this man!

(*Laughs soundlessly.*)

KING. Cardinal Grand Almoner! Lord Chancellor of the Crown! Lord High Keeper of the Royal Seal! I lift my hands up to you and ask your counsel!

GRAND ALMONER. (*laughs still more violently, but voiceless*) You have lost your war, Basilius. Vain was your war, untimely was your war, insolent and wicked was your war. And when it was lost, he who had raised his hands and had cried out against this war—he was driven from the council table. —For there was need of self-restraint, only thus was the war to be avoided—and of wisdom: and difficult is the path of wisdom, for it is full of thorns. But it was easy to do the deed of vanity, and rush out on horseback rather than sit and take counsel.

KING. Enough!

GRAND ALMONER. (*nods*) It is written: the depraved man does not love his punisher. The word *vain*, note this, Basilius, has a twofold sense. In one way it means: to boast of one's self, to be one's own spectator, to carry on a spiritual courtship with one's self. The other way it means: null and void, for nothing, lost in the mother's womb. —Vain was your thought, your deed, your begetting, nullified by yourself in the mother's womb.

KING. You basilisk! Oh that I could wrench the truth out of you, for you have always concealed the ultimate from me, like the malicious stepmother from the poor orphan.

GRAND ALMONER. The Truth, which is there behind all this show, abides with God.

KING. Is it then God or Satan who speaks through the stars? Answer me! —Do the stars lie?

GRAND ALMONER. Who are we that they should lie to us?

KING. I have put away my only son where no light shines
upon him. For it is prophesied that he will set his foot on
my neck in broad daylight and in full view of my people!

GRAND ALMONER. And you will wag your rump before him,
like a dog before his master, and you will desire to kiss the
butcher knife he takes you off with.

KING. Do you jeer at me? Do you not believe in prophecy?
Then answer me! How can they have seen what is not?
Where is the mirror that catches what was not there?

GRAND ALMONER. Just so! Hold to that which your eyes can
see, and amuse yourself with adulteresses and hounds! —But
I tell you: there is an eye beneath which today is like yesterday and tomorrow like today.

(*Moves closer to him*)

Therefore the future can be fathomed, and the sibyl stands
next to Solomon and the astrologer next to the prophet.

KING. (*under his breath*) I was sterile, however many virgins
and women I have known, and it was said: fertile in the
growing season with the queen, and my queen was with
child in the month of June. The child was born and he
tore the mother's womb, resisting the canny wife and the
physician. —He strove to be, naked out of nakedness,
deadly out of deadliness, and to fulfill the prophecy with
his first cry.—

GRAND ALMONER. And he is your child, got in holy matri-
mony!

KING. But I have never seen him and I must conceal myself
from him with bolts and chains and pikes and bars.

GRAND ALMONER. No one escapes the great ceremony, but
the king and the father are placed in the center.

KING. But now that I have rendered the creature harmless in
a tower with walls ten foot thick—and the rebellion shall
not come to a head—to what end—I demand of you!—to
what end has this insurrection come over my kingdom?

Shall I be the loser, by day and by night, and cheated of the glory of my empire and of the unspotted mirror of my conscience, of both at once? Are these sham skirmishes? Is God like the Duke of Lithuania who resorts to bluff?

GRAND ALMONER. Wonderfully joined are the tongs, edge to edge, and even the flaccid fruit when it is pressed gives a drop of oil!

KING. Be silent and hear me. I have commanded that the man who guards him shall be brought before me.

GRAND ALMONER. No! You have dared nothing in lifting the veil that was secured by all the terrors of majesty and guarded by tenfold threats of death!

KING. I have commanded that the man be brought who guards him and that he stand in my presence and in yours. And you, you will climb out of your wooden coffin and will preside in a tribunal over this boy whose face we have never seen. —Then it will be revealed whether he is a demon and a rebel out of the mother's womb: his head shall then fall and roll before your feet. Or else: I shall take my child into my arms, and the crown, a triple crown wrought into one, will not be without an heir. —Thereby will I know if God has appointed you my counsellor—or Satan.

GRAND ALMONER. God! God! do you pronounce the word with your dank lips? I shall teach you what that is, God! —You come to me for help and comfort, and you find what gives you no joy. In place of a trusted confidant to whom you show yourself as to a mirror, like the faces of those who cringe before you, you find a countenance unmoved which fills you with terror. Something there is that speaks through my mouth, but as if it came out of yourself and pointed at yourself; it does not hold you, and it does not release you; you do not proceed from one thing to another, rather one thing after another overtakes you: nothing new, nothing old, living through it but not fully

173

alive, waste, lame and yet turbulent. —You are no longer capable of action and attainment, dissolving but at the same time stone: naked in your need yet not free. But there is something else! You cry out: it is behind your cry, it compels you and bids you hear your own cry, feel your own body, weigh your body's heaviness, observe your body's gesture, like the welter of serpents with lashing tails, inhale your dissolution, smell your stench: ear behind ear, nose behind nose. It despairs behind your despair, horrifies you behind your horror and will not release you to yourself, for it knows you and means to punish you: that is God.

(*He sinks into himself with closed eyes.*)

KING. (*yells*) Advance my loyal men, take him. My chief minister owes me counsel and wants to defraud me of his debt!—

(*Courtiers rush in, monks appear, raise their hands in defense. The Grand Almoner lies back like a dead man.*)

CHOIR. "Ecce ego suscitabo super Babylonem quasi ventum pestilentem."

KING. (*turns away*) Carry him out.

(*Monks take the Grand Almoner up and bear him away. A knock on the gate. The gatekeeper unlocks it, lets in the Vaivode of Lublin and Julian as well as Gervasy and Protasy, behind them, Anton.*)

GERVASY and PROTASY. (*approach the king, bend their knee and announce*) The Vaivode of Lublin.

VAIVODE. (*steps before the king, bends his knee*) Your Highness forgive the delay. The roads are cut off by rebels. We had to move through the forests. I have brought the noble burgrave!

(*Julian steps up, kneels before the king.*)

KING. This one? His guardian?

(*He steps back suspiciously. Julian remains on his knees.*)

We graciously recall a former meeting.

(*Holds out his hand to be kissed, signals to rise*)

We shall know how to reward. —But we fear that we mark in your eye the reflected image of a demon.

JULIAN. (*rising to his feet, but with bent knee*) He is a gentle, handsome, well-made youth.

KING. Full of hatred inwardly?

JULIAN. Guileless. A blank white page.

KING. Human? Ah!

JULIAN. Oh! that it were your inscrutable will—

(*The king knits his brow, steps back.*)

JULIAN. —to subject the youth to a trial—

(*The king takes another step back.*)

JULIAN. Should he prove incapable, let him vanish again into the everlasting night of imprisonment.

KING. The dream of a night? Bold—and too bold! Who could give me assurance—

JULIAN. I! To your Majesty for everything! With this head!

KING. (*smiles*) A counsellor! At last, a true counsellor!—

(*with reference to the preceding; he beckons him to come up very close.*)

How many years have you performed your difficult office?

JULIAN. Twenty-two years less one month. His age.

KING. Unexampled! Learn, my grandees, learn what devotion is. Twenty-two years!

JULIAN. (*bends over the proffered hand; he too has tears in his eyes.*) They are in this instant extinguished.

(*Anton approaches from behind, unnoticed; he pricks up his ears.*)

KING. Meeting you again has moved us deeply. It is your arms that shield our kin.

(*He draws him close, with the gesture of an embrace.*)

How would we bear it, were he himself—

(*His face changes, but only for a moment.*)

A loyal man near at hand, what a treasure! Counsellor, comforter! You have given me back my life.

(*Beckons to Julian confidentially*)

You will follow us to court. We have much to discuss, in confidence.

(*Julian bows to the ground. The king signals to the gate-keeper who unlocks the gate. Courtiers approach Julian. Anton tries inconspicuously to get closer to his master.*)

A COURTIER. (*with a slight bow*) We are close relations. Your Lordship's grandmother was my honored grandfather's sister. I would hope that your Lordship had not perhaps become unmindful of this during the years in which your Lordship was not seen at court.

(*Anton pricks up his ears.*)

TWO OTHERS. (*in the same manner*) Sir, grant us your protection. We would die my Lord's ever ready and most obliged servants!

YOUNG CHAMBERLAIN. (*stepping up to Julian, with a deep reverence*) I kiss your hands, Excellency!

(*All leave.*)

Scene 2

(*Inside the tower. Pentagonal room with a narrow barred window. In a back corner, a small iron door. On the wall a large crucifix. A wooden bench, a pail, a washbasin. In the background Sigismund sits on some half-burnt straw. He wears a clean-looking suit made of heavy cotton; his feet are bare, but without chains. The door is being unlocked from the outside.*)

ANTON. (*enters. He takes a broom, which leans next to the door, sprinkles the floor with water from the pail and begins to sweep. Sigismund looks at him, but is silent.*)

ANTON. (*while sweeping, he sniffs the air*) What's that? You've been kindling fire in the straw? A heap of straw burnt up, and sprigs, everything! —God's mercy, if a guard had caught you. —What have you been doing, and why?

SIGISMUND. (*quickly*) My father was in the fire.

ANTON. Then what did he look like? A face of fire, a coat of smoke, a bluish-glowing paunch and red hot shoes?

SIGISMUND. (*turns his head away*) My father has no face!

ANTON. You've got bats in your—

(*Sprinkles holy water over him from a small leaden basin which hangs on the wall underneath the crucifix*)

Tidy up now! Aren't you a human creature? Human kind is disgusted when a place looks like the devil's bedchamber.

SIGISMUND. (*anxiously*) Anton, what is that: human—as I am, human kind?

ANTON. (*pours water into the basin for him*) Here now, wash your face, and that will put different thoughts in your head.

(*The sound of the door being unlocked from the outside.*)

Here's a towel.

(*Throws a gay-colored cotton cloth towards him; Sigismund wipes his face.*)

And now! Look there! They're coming for you!

(*From the outside the iron door has been opened. A countrywoman, Sigismund's foster mother, has entered; she remains standing near the door. Sigismund turns his face to the wall.*)

COUNTRYWOMAN. (*comes closer, to Anton*) Is he sick? Does he have his senses about him?

(*Sigismund hides head and hands in the straw.*)

COUNTRYWOMAN. Seven years that I have not seen him. Is't true he has grown claws? Burning eyes, like the night fowl?

ANTON. A lie! Show your hands, Sigismund. —There he is, look at him!

SIGISMUND. (*collects himself*) Mother, have you come to me?

COUNTRYWOMAN. (*advances*) Your hair is a tangle. Where's your comb? Give it to me so I can comb it.

(*Anton hands her a leaden comb from a wall shelf.*)

COUNTRYWOMAN. (*combs Sigismund's hair*)
Image of God, watch over yourself. Don't you recall how the countrywomen used to spy through the fence because of your white cheeks and raven-black hair? Used to put milk and honey outside the gate, I had to hide you away, board up the window shutters! Strict was the order!

SIGISMUND. Where is your husband?

COUNTRYWOMAN. Your foster father is dead these four years. Pray with me for his soul.

SIGISMUND. But where is my soul?

COUNTRYWOMAN. How? What is it you are asking?

SIGISMUND. I ask justly. Do you remember still, the pig that father slaughtered—it shrieked so hard, and I shrieked too. Then it hung from the cross beam, in the hall, close by my door; I could look deep into its inside. Was that the soul which fled out of it when it shrieked so frightfully, and is my soul gone into the dead animal instead?

COUNTRYWOMAN. (*prays*) Our Father which art in heaven—

SIGISMUND. Where is my own father that he abandoned me! Although he made me!

COUNTRYWOMAN. (*points to the crucifix*) There is your Father and your Redeemer! Look on him, there! —Imprint his likeness on your heart, stamp it in, like mold and die!

SIGISMUND. (*looks at it for a long time, mimics the posture, with spread-out arms; then he lets his arms sink*)
I cannot keep it asunder, myself with him there and then again myself with the animal which was hung up on a cross beam and black with blood inside. Mother, what is the end of me and the end of that animal?

(*He closes his eyes.*)

COUNTRYWOMAN. Open your eyes! Look at him! Forsaken by his Father in heaven! Crowned with thorns, beaten with rods, spit at, in the face, by the soldier-men! Keep your eyes on it. —Look there, obstinate boy!

SIGISMUND. (*cries out*) Mother, do not make me angry!

(*He pushes her from him.*)

COUNTRYWOMAN. (*folds her hands, in prayer*)
O you fourteen holy saints and helpers-in-need, you strong warriors and servants of God, glorified and crowned with golden crowns, draw near to help this boy, help him turn his mind from gnashing teeth, clenched fists; better that

you caused his hands to drop off, his feet to get lame, his eyes to get blind, his ears to get deaf and defend his soul from the violent deed and from evil. Amen.

(*She makes the sign of the cross over him.*)

SIGISMUND. (*cries fearfully*) Mother!

(*In the back, the door has again been unlocked, and Julian has entered. In the door another person becomes visible who waits. The countrywoman bows, and kisses Julian's coat. Julian remains standing. —Sigismund flees to his bed of straw.*)

JULIAN. Is this how you have calmed him? Has the woman not been able to do better? and you—

(*steps closer*)

Sigismund, I have come to visit you.

(*Beckons, Anton brings him a low wooden stool on which he sits.*)

I have come to bring you joy, Sigismund. Attend to what my lips will now say: you have passed a long, difficult time of trial. Do you understand what I say?

(*Sigismund conceals his hands under his sleeves.*)

JULIAN. Are you listening to me?
SIGISMUND. You have supreme power over me. I tremble before you. I know that I cannot escape you.

(*Instinctively he conceals his hands.*)

I look upon your hands and your mouth that I may rightly understand your will.
JULIAN. Power is given from above. From someone higher than I am, note this well. But I was your rescuer. Secretly

I poured oil into the lamp of your life; because of me alone there is still light in you. Remember that. —Do I seem so strange to you, Sigismund? Did I not let you sit next to me at a wooden table and open before you the great book and pointed in it figure after figure to the things of the world and called them by name for you and have I not thereby singled you out from among your equals?

(*Sigismund remains silent.*)

JULIAN. Have I not told you of Moses with the tablets and Noah in the ark and Gideon with his sword and David with the harp, of Rome, that great and mighty city and her emperors, and that from them are descended our illustrious kings? Have I not taught you the meaning of master and servant, of distance and nearness, of guilt and punishment, of heavenly and earthly? Answer me!

(*Sigismund stares fixedly on the ground.*)

SIGISMUND. Unlike the beast, I understand my ignorance. I have knowledge of what I do not see, I know what is far from me. Therefore I suffer torment like no other creature.

JULIAN. Excellent privilege! Thank me! For thus the lips of man become potent because he endows the letter with spirit, calling and commanding! —Why do you groan?

SIGISMUND. Still there is one fearful word: which outweighs all the others!

JULIAN. What kind of word is that? What is it called, this word? I am eager to hear what magic word it is!

SIGISMUND. Sigismund!

(*He runs his fingers over his cheeks and down his body.*)

Who is that: I? Where does it end? Who called me so first? Father? Mother? Show them to me!

JULIAN. Your parents have cast you off. You were guilty before them.

SIGISMUND. Loathsome is the animal. It eats its own young still moist from the mother's womb. My eyes have seen it. And yet it is guiltless.

JULIAN. Search not out these things until the veil is rent. Stand firm upon your self! Alone! I have so endowed you! Spirit of light, before whom angels kneel! Son of fire, supreme! First born!

SIGISMUND. Why is your speech so grand? What are you waving in your hand that sparkles so and glows?

JULIAN. That which stag and eagle and serpent thirst for: that they might with plants and minerals, with draughts and waters renew their life: for the chosen one is born twice. Flaming air I wield in my hand, elixir of a new life, freedom healing like balsam! Drink this and live!

(Sigismund recoils from the vial in Julian's hand.)

ANTON. Hurrah! Sigismund! We go on a journey! Large is the world! Up with you, out of the straw!

SIGISMUND. Must I go back into total darkness! Young as I am! Woe to me! my blood will then be upon you!

JULIAN. Into the light! So close to the light that only a young eagle would not go blind. —Drink this.

SIGISMUND. You have taught me yourself that they pardon prisoners with a draught.

(Julian has stepped to the door, and beckoned. A masked servant, who holds a cup, has entered. Julian takes the cup, pours from the vial, and puts it again into his belt pocket. The servant disappears.)

JULIAN. Drink this!

SIGISMUND. *(falls down before him)* Tell me first who I am?

ANTON. They'll tell you, surely, soon as you arrive, some-

where! Only, don't ask too many questions beforehand, it
makes people contrary! Drink it down, quick!

JULIAN. (*hands Sigismund the draught*)
You are you. Hear me: The world is subject to deeds. Do
you know what deeds are? Drink and behold.

SIGISMUND. Help me, Anton!

JULIAN. Shall my men lay hold of you with their hands? I
will call them—you there, advance!

(*He is near the door.*)

ANTON. (*kneels down next to Sigismund*) Let him but live,
your Lordship, spare his life only!

SIGISMUND. (*takes the cup and drinks from it rapidly*)
While you speak harshly, I have drunk it for your sake.

(*He takes a few steps to the rear and sits on the ground
after giving the cup to Anton.*)

ANTON. (*drops the cup*) I must hold up his head, he shall not
die leaning against hard rock.

JULIAN (*restrains him*) Silence, fool! Who speaks of dying?
Now he begins to live.

ANTON. (*kneels next to Sigismund, strokes his feet*) Doesn't
your Lordship see, then, he has a halo above his face! O my
saintly blessed martyrized—

JULIAN. Silence and call in the servants!

ANTON. (*walks toward the iron door which stands ajar*)
They're already here!

(*Two masked servants have quietly entered and remain
standing near the door.*)

SIGISMUND. (*to Julian and Anton, but as if to strangers*)
I feel very light. All my fear is quite gone. Only my feet
are getting cold. Warm them, Anton.

ANTON. (*close to him*) You know me then?

SIGISMUND. Raise them into the fiery furnace in which walk the young men, singing, my brothers: O Lord God, we praise you! Face to face! Chosen!

(*He throws his hands upwards.*)

Father—I come—

(*falls back senseless. The two masked servants step forward.*)

JULIAN. The robes made ready? The shoes, the belt, everything? Put on his garments, with courtesy and respect!

(*The servants take Sigismund up.*)

JULIAN. (*has spread a cloak over him, then to Anton*) The carriage to be ready and harnessed! The escort prepared to mount! The guard stand to arms. Give the signal! Move on!

(*Anton pulls out a kerchief, runs out. The servants carry Sigismund out. Julian follows. Trumpet signal outside.*)

JULIAN. (*beckons Olivier to him.*)

(*Olivier removes his cap which had served as a mask.*)

JULIAN. You and your fellow take the nearer road. Wherever we should meet, you do not know me. You will take up quarters on the edge of town and make contacts with malcontents, tax evaders, deserters.

OLIVIER. That's already done. The fellowship of unbelievers and debtors has been notified.

JULIAN. Who gave you permission to act beforehand?

OLIVIER. (*slily*)

I am a dragon with many tails. One must make use of my person according to its nature.

JULIAN. (*steps closely up to him*)

Must?

ANTON. (*running in*) He's lying in the carriage. Everything is ready to mount.

JULIAN. In God's name.

(*He goes out. One more trumpet signal outside.*)

CURTAIN

ACT III

(*The death chamber of the queen, in the royal castle. A tall window in the background. In the right wall an alcove with the bed, which can be screened off by a curtain. On the left in front an oratory from which one can look down into the church. In the center of the left wall, opposite the entrance door, a fireplace. From the oratory a secret door leads into a narrow passageway part of which is just visible in the left wing of the stage. The window shutters are closed. An eternal light burns in the alcove. The castellan unlocks the door from the outside and enters with two servants; they open only one wing of the main door. The servants open the wooden shutters of the tall window in the back: outside it is broad daylight.*)

CASTELLAN. (*clanking the large ring of keys*) The death chamber of her late majesty the queen! No one has entered here by this main door in twenty-one years. The reverend sisters of the Visitation, two of whom remain here in prayer from midnight till dawn, they come in by this small door; it leads down a winding staircase, hidden inside the pillar, right into the sacristy.

(*From below the sound of the organ and the singing voices of nuns become audible. The castellan goes to the alcove, sprinkles holy water on the bed out of a silver basin near*

185

the entrance to the alcove, then draws the curtain reverently. Approaching human voices can be heard outside. Then three strokes of a halberd against the stone floor. The castellan signals, the servants run to the door and open both wings wide. The court enters: trabants, mace-bearers, pages with tapers. Then the bearer of the imperial standard with the silver eagle, followed by a page who carries upon a crimson cushion the king's prayer book and gloves. The king, wearing a curved saber and his Polish hat in his hand. Close on his heels, his confessor. Courtiers in pairs, preceded by Julian walking alone; behind the courtiers, four chamberlains. Lastly the physician with his assistant—a young man with spectacles—behind him Anton who carries a covered silver basin. —The king halts in the center of the room, holds out his hat. A page rushes forward, takes the hat on bent knee. The king takes his gloves off the cushion, which the kneeling page holds up to him, puts on the left glove, tucks the right one in his belt. The trabants and the mace-bearers have moved around the room and out again through the double door, also the castellan and the servants. The door is closed. Two mace-bearers post themselves inside the door. The gentlemen of the court stand in front of the oratory, Julian farthest to the right. The physician and his assistant stop next to the door. The king steps toward the alcove. A chamberlain hastens to pull the curtain back. Another chamberlain hands the king the aspergillum. The king sprinkles holy water on the bed, then kneels and remains for a moment in prayer. The confessor kneels down with him. The king rises, steps into the center, the confessor a little to his side and behind him. The singing and the music of the organ have stopped.)

KING. (*to the confessor*) I have prayed before the death bed of my wife, blessed be her memory, for me and for him. This short prayer has wonderfully refreshed my soul.

(He beckons to the physician.)

You persist in your wish to withdraw?

PHYSICIAN. Your majesty has granted me this one condition, that I be spared from standing myself in the presence of the prince, should the need arise to administer a drug again. My assistant is completely informed, that is, about the procedures which may be necessary—not about the facts of the case.

(In a lower voice)

He looks upon the prince as a mentally disordered person in whom your majesty because of distant kinship takes an interest. May it all turn out—I have prepared a sponge dipped in essence of unfailing strength. The servant there keeps it in a covered dish. He has been close to the prisoner; if necessary, he can be of help. May these preparations prove to be superfluous, I pray God.

KING. That has been our incessant prayer these last nine days and nights. —You have grown very close to us in our esteem in these days. We regard your illustrious person from this moment as our loyal and sworn physician in ordinary.

(Holds out his right hand to be kissed; the physician bends over it, then goes to the door, which is opened by a mace-bearer. The physician leaves; at the door he bows once again.)

KING. Strengthen me continually with your advice, reverend father. —I have allowed my counsellors to persuade me. —I have submitted my tender human nature to higher judgment.

CONFESSOR. Even Holy Scripture—

KING. I know, the pagans too. Even the pagans. They did not scruple; their own sons—

CONFESSOR. In one day the consul had the heads of two sons laid before their feet.

KING. Two! in one day! What were his reasons?

CONFESSOR. To render satisfaction to the offended law.

KING. How? to the law? the law? But—

CONFESSOR. The law and the sovereign are one.

KING. Paternal authority—the father is the creator—his power directly derived—

CONFESSOR. From the power of God the creator, the source of all that is.

KING. (*takes one step away from the courtiers, draws the confessor after him*) And the absolution, if I find myself forced to have him brought back there, again—my own son—there again where the light of the sun does not shine on him—?

CONFESSOR. You have doubts? To prevent incalculable evil!

(*From the outside a scraping on the door.*)

CHAMBERLAIN. (*goes to the door, speaks with someone through the half-opened wing. He then approaches the king, and on bent knee whispers to him.*)

KING. (*makes a sign.*)

(*Mace-bearer opens the door, lets Gervasy and Protasy come in. Gervasy and Protasy hasten towards the king, bend their knee.*)

KING. (*inclines his ear to Gervasy who whispers.*)
This youth rides his horse nobly like a cavalier?

(*He looks at Julian severely.*)

JULIAN. He has never in his life mounted a horse. I have always been mindful of the strict prohibition.

PROTASY. (*meanwhile whispers into the king's other ear.*)

KING (*sternly to Julian*) Those whom we have appointed his followers he does not deign to notice with a single glance!

What manner of speech is to be expected when he stands in our presence?

JULIAN. Perhaps the speech that angels speak. His words are the issue of an inward source—as in a blazed tree which discharges even through its wound a balmy sap.

(*Gervasy and Protasy, bending their knee, withdraw.*)

KING. (*to Julian, softly*) Has this boy been impressed with the supreme concept of authority? the concept of absolute obedience?

(*He looks at him severely.*)

JULIAN. (*steady under his eye*) Consider, my king, that the youth does not know this world, nor his position in it. He knows one Supreme Being: he lifts his eyes to the stars and his soul to God.

KING. We will hope that this is enough.

(*Very audible*)

For the world is out of hand, and we are determined to quench the spreading flames—and if need be in rivers of blood.

(*The courtiers who stand in the rear near the window gaze down. The pages crowd around the window and seek with some commotion to look down. The king notices this and turns to look.*)

CHAMBERLAIN. The prince is dismounting. He turns toward the portal and steps inside the castle.

KING. (*to Julian, controlling himself with an effort*) I do not yet wish to see him.

(*He conducts Julian away from the courtiers, to the front.*)

A great moment, a terrible decisive moment.

JULIAN. (*falls on his knees*) His words sound at times violent and rash—consider, your majesty, in your wisdom and for-bearance: the creature has never had a friend.

KING. I too have never had a friend about me.

JULIAN. (*on his knees*) His youthful foot has never taken one step without a heavy bestial chain!

KING. I too, Count Julian, have never taken a free step.

JULIAN. (*on his knees*) Show forbearance, great prince, to this sorely tried creature!

KING. (*looks at him*) Be always his counsellor, my wise Julian, gentler to him than mine has been to me. —I hold you in great esteem—I am almost ashamed to show how much!

(*He takes the golden chain with the white eagle set with diamonds off his neck and hangs it around Julian's, pronouncing*)

Sic nobis placuit!

(*Holds out his hand to be kissed by Julian, and raises him.*)

(*With an altered expression*)

And this ever restless people? This half-stifled yet ever smoldering insurrection? What do you think of it? You have your connections everywhere, your restless hands reach everywhere—

(*He looks at him suspiciously.*)

JULIAN. (*tries to speak*) My king—

KING. These secret fellowships—these sinister alliances shunning the light? —I am informed.

JULIAN. But *one* princely gesture—with *one* act, my king—

KING. You suppose we will overthrow them easily if we give you full authority?

JULIAN. It is easy for a great king to regain the confidence of his people.

KING. Ah, you mean that I must regain *their* confidence—not they mine?

(*He stares at him fixedly.*)

JULIAN. Both, my king, both will come to be in one.

KING. When I have abdicated?

JULIAN. God forbid! —Your mildness towards the one will subdue all hearts. Each will feel himself singly overcome with gratitude—to see such a fount of grace flow forth.

KING. O cause for gratitude—he will have it. And my people too. —If I could discover to you my inmost self.

(*The organ becomes again audible, but without the singing voices.*)

KING. (*beckons to one of the courtiers*) Assemble the court outside.

(*The mace-bearers open the door, the pages run out, the mace-bearers follow. The two young chamberlains and several courtiers withdraw. —The king joins the group which is left. The castellan has come in with the keys and hands them, bowing, to the eldest courtier; he goes out again.*)

KING. You, my most trusted companions, bound to me by sacred oaths—wait there, inside. The antechamber, even where the intimate company of the queen used to gather before mass—stay in there. What I have to say to the prince is not meant for witnesses. But if I step onto the dais with my young guest and as a sign of accord place a father's arm around his shoulder, then let the trumpets sound: because then a great hour has come for this kingdom.

(*The courtiers bow and leave. They can be seen going through the secret door of the oratory into the small passageway and withdrawing to the left: all except the father confessor. They are followed by the physician's assistant, and behind him Anton.*)

ANTON. (*in passing, to Julian*) I dreamt of muddy water! It will end badly.

KING. (*beckons to the father confessor to wait, then calls Julian with a wink of his eye*)
Those words of my late honored great uncle, the Emperor Charles the Fifth, with which he gave his crown and lands to his only son, Don Philip, now rise before my soul.

JULIAN. (*kneels and kisses his hand*) May his soul reveal itself to you. Does not the crystal attain its noble form under terrible pressure? Thus will he be when your eye discerns him truly.

KING. Perhaps I too will retire into a monastery for the remainder of my days—may a worthy son repay my subjects what he deems owing to me in gratitude.

(*His face is altered; he beckons to the confessor. Julian steps back.*)

KING. (*to the confessor, quickly*) But where runs the borderline that must not be crossed, where transgression would —before God and the world—justify the extremest harshness? Where, my father? —You are silent. If he were to raise his hand against me?

CONFESSOR. God forbid!

KING. Some will say even then: the victim of the reason of state had not been master of his disordered senses.

CONFESSOR. Wise judges, my king, have passed the verdict: a five-year old boy becomes punishable and can be deprived of life by the sword insofar as he knows how to choose between an apple offered to him and a copper penny.

KING. (*smiles*) A five-year old child! Most wisely thought out! A wonderful paradigm! A prince who sits on horseback like a born king and in his pride does not condescend to address his noble followers is at any rate no five-year old child.

CHAMBERLAIN. (*comes quickly through the door on the right, announces kneeling*) They are coming!

KING. Who is with him?

CHAMBERLAIN. The prince with an imperious gesture bade his gentlemen-in-waiting to remain behind. Count Adam alone, bound in duty, has followed him and escorts him up the stairs.

KING. Away with you, in there. To the others. You too, reverend father.

(*Confessor and chamberlain leave. To Julian*)

You stay!

(*The confessor, and behind him the chamberlain, can be seen going off through the passageway. Then the king and Julian step into the passage and remain standing, visible. They look through the window into the room. The room remains empty for one second, then the young chamberlain, Count Adam, appears in the opening door: he holds it open from the outside. He lets Sigismund enter, comes in behind him, and closes the door. Sigismund is splendidly attired, but does not carry a weapon in his belt. He enters, looks about him; then steps to the window and looks out: then again to the middle of the room.*)

KING. (*visible next to Julian, looks on, outside the room*) Noble! princely in his every gesture!

(*He supports himself on Julian.*)

KING. The very image of my wife! Armed against every means of approach with absolute dumb impossibility.

(*To Julian*)

Go in! and prepare him! entirely! Tell him everything!

JULIAN. (*softly*) Everything, even to the last point?

KING. (*overcome by tears*) Even the last! And then open the door for me and leave me with him, alone. Go!

(*Julian steps through the secret door into the oratory and from there into the room. The organ sounds for a moment a little louder, thereafter it is now and then softly audible. The chamberlain notices him first, steps back and bows. Upon a sign from Julian he goes to the door, makes a low bow once more in the direction of Sigismund and leaves. Sigismund turns his head, sees Julian, draws himself suddenly up, and turns his back to Julian. He trembles violently.*)

JULIAN. (*three paces behind Sigismund, goes down on one knee. He also can barely master his emotion. Softly*) Prince Sigismund!

(*Sigismund raises his hands in a gesture of defense, as if imploring, but without turning toward Julian, with a low hardly audible sound of terror.*)

JULIAN. Yes, I.

(*Silence.*)

This was the journey which I promised you. This house is its destination.

(*Sigismund quickly looks behind, but immediately turns his back to him again.*)

KING. How he screws his eyes up at him, from below. He hates him obviously. This is manna for my soul!

JULIAN. (*rises and speaks from the same distance*)
You have said to yourself that it is your father who thus governs over you. You comprehend that your father's ways had to be inscrutable to you as were your ways to the animals. You would not wish to live unless someone

higher were above you, that is the sense of your thinking.
—You do not ask: What has happened to me?—

SIGISMUND. (*shakes his head.*)

JULIAN. Nor: Why has it happened to me?—

SIGISMUND. (*shakes his head.*)

JULIAN. For your heart is not vain. You respect power which
is above you; you are ever aware of something higher because you are yourself of the highest. And now, are you
ready?

SIGISMUND. (*hides his hands.*)

JULIAN. Stay. Do not hide your hands. Show them without
dread. Hold this fast in your mind: I am your father's
servant. A man recalls with each breath that which is above
him.

KING. (*outside, but visible, kneels down and prays*)
Work a miracle, Lord in heaven! and reconcile him to his
fate whose innocent tool I have been. Amen.

(*His face, as he rises again, streams with tears.*)

JULIAN. (*having looked around*)
Sigismund, crown prince of Poland, Duke of Gotland, I
have to announce to you the visit of your royal father.

SIGISMUND. (*falls on his knees, covers his face with his hands.
Julian hurries to the door, opens it and lets the king enter.
The organ music becomes softer. The king stands in the
room; Sigismund is still on his knees, his face in his hands,
even as his father stands before him. Julian goes out into
the passageway, disappears to the left.*)

(*The organ now sounds stronger, the music swells might-
ily; the* vox humana *stands out strongly.*)

SIGISMUND. (*stands as if deprived of his senses, then his eyes
search where this sound originates; he looks up, trembles
violently. Tears rush to his eyes.*)

KING. (*after a pause*) Speak my son, let me hear your voice.

SIGISMUND. (*down on his knees, his head toward the ground.*)

KING. My son, we have forgiven you. You have returned home. Our arms are open. Let us see your countenance!

SIGISMUND. (*trembles, starts convulsively; he turns his head towards the wall; kneels down, there, his face averted. He presses his face against the wall.*)

KING. No, it rests with us. We humble ourselves before him who has suffered. We bow down.

(*He bows slightly.*)

SIGISMUND. (*trembles more violently, conceals his head behind a chair.*)

KING. Like Saint Martin as he came upon the beggar, naked and shivering with cold—

(*He grasps his sword.*)

Look up! Shall we divide our royal cloak with you? or

(*he pushes the sword back into the sheath*)

will you come to our heart, into its undivided warmth?

(*He opens his arms.*)

SIGISMUND. (*stands up.*)

KING. Let us hear your voice, young prince! We desire it. We have missed its sound too long.

SIGISMUND. (*speaks, but no sound issues from his lips.*)

KING. What do you whisper to yourself? May it be a good spirit that whispers from within you!

SIGISMUND. (*cannot speak.*)

KING. Your eye upon ours! Hearken, Poland's Heir, once for all! We can do no wrong, as king to the subject, as father to the son; and if we had placed your head without trial upon the block, then the sacred power was bestowed upon us, and there is no one who could find fault with us. For we were before you—therefore you are delivered into our hand by God Himself.

SIGISMUND. (*shows by signs that he is afraid of power, afraid of the king's hands. He groans.*)

From where—so much power?

KING. (*smiles*) Only the fullness of power profits: in the midst of which we sit, peerless, solitary. Such is the power of the king. All other is borrowed from it and is a semblance.

SIGISMUND. From where, so much power? from where?

KING. From God directly. From the Father whom you know. On the day when it pleased God—did we step into our right as heir. The herald's proclamation resounded into the four winds, the crown touched the anointed head, this cloak was placed around our shoulders. And there was again a king in Poland. What is it? What ails you?

SIGISMUND. Then reveal your secret to me, even now! Uncover your face before me!

(*His eyes are very close to the face of the king; he steps back.*)

KING. (*stares at him fixedly.*)

SIGISMUND. I have never kissed anyone. Give me the kiss of peace, my father!

KING. Enough. I do not like such words. Come to your senses, Prince of Poland. Remember whence I, your king, have called you and to what heights I have raised you.

SIGISMUND. Raised? Do you raise me now above myself and up to you? Yes? —Uncover your face. Give yourself to me as you have taken me. Mother, father! take me to you.

KING. The desire for power consumes you. I can read it in your features. —But you were taught to win hearts with words of sentiment.

(*With an ironic smile*)

May such talents profit you after my death. —But now sit here at my feet, my son.

(*He sits on a high seat, Sigismund at his feet on a low stool.*)

In me put your trust and in no one else. —Of one thing kings have need: to learn how to guard themselves against their evil counsellors. They are vipers at our breast. Do you hear me, my son? Answer me.

SIGISMUND. I hear, my father.

KING. (*looks into his face*) Do you hear? I look for child-like devotion in your eyes, and I do not find it. You are withdrawn, my son. You are sly and self-confident. —Good. I see you are equal to any enterprise. —I will entrust you with the first and greatest.

(*He rises, Sigismund too.*)

KING. Set us free from the serpent Julian, who has entangled us both.

SIGISMUND. What, father? What says my father?

KING. (*in the direction of Sigismund's hand*) How, my father? What?

(*Suddenly, terribly*)

Held in chains? the heir to three crowns under his whip? and pretended to me you were wild? My days poisoned, my nights made hollow with the horrible tale of a raving boy with murderous eyes! with the ghost of a born rebel!—

(*Altering his tone*)

And to what end? You sense it, my poor son? To chain you to him joined by the wrong done to me—to make him your lord and master forever—debasing you to be-

come the tool of your own tool—to make a second Basilius
of you, and a second Ignatius of himself—

(*he gnashes his teeth wildly*)

if you do not prevent him.—

SIGISMUND. (*looks at him terrified, covers his face with his
hands.*)

KING. Closer to me!

(*Softly*)

What is this common revolt with the threat of which he
now again assails my unsuspecting heart!

SIGISMUND. What revolt! I know of no revolt!

KING. (*draws him close to himself*) I do not ask you: who
has been stirring up this insurrection in my lands for the
last year? in whose hand, if not in his, do these threads run
together? Quiet!

(*He puts his hand over Sigismund's mouth.*)

I am not questioning you. I do not wish that you surrender
your teacher to me. I surrender him to you.

SIGISMUND. You surrender him to me? my teacher? He has
taught me to read in a book. He has taught me everything.

KING. Let his fate be in your hands. Quiet. Take this ring.
I place it upon your finger.

SIGISMUND. This ring!

KING. Whoever wears it is lord and master. My guards obey
him. My ministers execute his commands. Go forth out of
my arms and strike like lightning. Let your first deed be
sudden, terrifying, bewildering!

SIGISMUND. My first deed! I imagined it when I swung the
horse bone over vermin—do not recall it!

KING. (*close to his ear*) Arrest this traitor Julian and see
whether this plotted rebellion does not wither like a bundle
of sprigs!

SIGISMUND. (*speechless.*)

KING. (*draws him nearer*) With this look, which you cast at me now, step in front of him. The prerogatives of this ring on your hand are immeasurable. They make you equal to me, my son.

SIGISMUND. Your equal? Your power—is now here?—

(He holds the ring in front of him.)

KING. (*softly, confidentially*) They place the grip of the hangman's axe directly in the hand of the trabant who goes with you on a night-time errand. There is also from now on only one king in Poland—

SIGISMUND. Only one!

KING. But he appears in two shapes, and one of them is new and terrible. Woe to our enemies!

(He pushes him gently away.)

Go! go!

SIGISMUND. (*steps back*) What are you, Satan, who cheats me of father and mother?

(He strikes him in the face.)

KING. Trabants! In here! On your knees, reckless fool!

SIGISMUND. (*takes hold of him*) What, do you bare your teeth? Why does your face look so mean? —Once before I have had to strangle an old fox with my hands! He smelled like you.

(Thrusts him away.)

KING. Down on your knees, rebellious beast! When! Does no one answer! We will chastise you! We will not shrink from dragging you along the ground in front of the people, and up the headman's block!

SIGISMUND. I am here now! —My will! There is nothing of

woman in me! My hair is short and it bristles. I show my claws. This moment, to your horror, has born me.

KING. Untouchable! Sovereign Majesty! Help, here!

(*He turns to the left; Sigismund cuts him off.*)

PAGE. (*from the left*) The king calls!

SIGISMUND. (*presses hard upon the king, pulls his sword out of the sheath, brandishing it*)

I command! Over there! Down on the ground! I will tread upon you! —Since I am here, I am king! Else, why did you bring me here?

KING. (*groans under his grip.*)

SIGISMUND. Bellow! Make an uproar! Call out! Scream yourself to death! Off with your cloak!

KING. (*tries to escape. Julian appears in the passageway, left, rushes in and out again through the door on the right. Sigismund runs after the king with drawn sword. The king collapses. Sigismund tears the cloak off him and hangs it around his shoulders. Pages in the passage, left, cry out: "Help!" Several courtiers rush in, make their way through the oratory into the room. The passageway is crowded with courtiers, chamberlains, pages. All cry out in confusion: "Who calls? What has happened? In here! It is forbidden! The king is dead!" —Those who have rushed into the room keep to the left.*)

SIGISMUND. (*his eyes fixed on them*)

Silence! Not one look at the old corpse! On your knees, all of you! Kiss the ground at the feet of your new master and throw the ancient carcass there into the ditch—move there! The first two in front!

(*The courtiers remain motionless. Behind them several have moved into the room. The door on the right opens, Julian's head appears. He looks in all directions, then leaps into the room. He holds the royal banner tightly against his body, throws himself down on his knees in front of Sigismund, and handing the banner over, he calls out: "Long live the King.")*

SIGISMUND. (*grasps the banner with his left hand*)

Come in here, you! Here, look on your lord! Prepare yourselves! I shall clean house here like a hawk in the hencoop! My deeds will do justice to my will. Understand me right. My power will reach as far as my will. On your knees!

(*He throws the naked sword at their feet.*)

There! I do not need that! I am master here!

(*Several in front kneel down.*)

COUNT ADAM. (*among the courtiers cries out*)

The king lives! Assist his majesty!

(*He tears the standard from Sigismund's hand.*)

There is but one king in Poland! *Vivat* Basilius!

(*Two chamberlains move cautiously along the left wall and get in back of Sigismund. One throws his arms from behind around Sigismund and brings him down. Several others now fall upon him, too. He is half dragged, half carried into the alcove. The elder courtiers and the pages hasten towards the king, and help him rise. Pages bring the cloak from the back and place it around his shoulders. The confessor supports him. At the same time a voice from the alcove: "He is down!" Another voice: "Call the physician!" —The assistant of the physician and Anton with the covered dish next to him are the last to step out of the oratory. The assistant goes to the alcove where he is being called. He looks around for Anton, who clasps the covered dish against his body. Several persons come running, pull the dish out of Anton's hands, carry it quickly towards the alcove. The king has risen to his feet.*)

KING. (*trembles*) It has happened as it was prophesied. He set his foot upon me in view of the people. —But we have remained in possession of our crown and can decree his punishment! Ah! who would have dared to hope for that! I am thirsty.

A COURTIER. A draught for the king!

(Several pages run out.)

KING. *(touches his right hand with the left)*
My ring!

(Someone runs to the bed, brings the ring, hands it over on his knees.)

KING. It too must be washed clean in blood.

(Looks at it. He beckons several of them to approach.)

A frenzy must have taken hold of the common people! They lie prostrate in the churches, I hear, and pray for a new king, an innocent boy, who will come in chains and bring on a new kingdom. —We will give them a wholesome spectacle. The scaffold shall go up in the center of the great market square, higher than any that has ever been erected. Three times twenty steps shall he climb till he find the block whereon to lay his head.

(Louder, addressing all of them)

I wish to see the people of my capital city, each rank and station, ceremoniously invited, and they that are chained in the mines and on the galleys shall be set free. They shall be lined up in clean holiday robes, and he shall also be led past them in order that even the lowest of my subjects will not be left without a diversion on such a festive day.

(The door opens.)

TWO PAGES. Room for the king's draught!

(Three pipers playing. —The chief cupbearer. The goblet, carried by a page.)

CHIEF CUPBEARER. (*kneeling, hands the goblet to the king, rises again, and as the king touches his lips to the goblet calls out*)

The king is drinking!

ALL. Hail to Your Majesty!

(*The chief cupbearer on his knees receives the empty goblet, goes out with the pipers and pages.*)

KING. (*rises*) The physician! We are in need of his skill. The creature shall atone under the sword, being of sound mind and body!

PAGES. (*go out.*)

KING. (*takes a few steps.*)

COURTIERS. (*move aside and reveal to view: Julian against the wall surrounded by three of them who hold their drawn daggers pointed at him.*)

JULIAN. (*with closed eyes, groans.*)

ANTON. (*near him*) Oh my, do you feel so poorly? Does your Lordship need to be let blood?

KING. (*keeps his eye on him, whispers to a courtier. Three pages stand nearby.*)

COURTIER. Pages, do your duty!

PAGES. (*fall upon Julian, rip the chain of the order off him and pull the royal seal from his belt.*)

JULIAN. Stand, now! Walk upright out of here!

(*He collapses.*)

PHYSICIAN. (*enters rapidly and goes towards the king.*)

KING. Not here! —We have even now defended ourself alone against a very serious assault. There you are needed. And his accomplice too must soon regain his senses for me. In these next three days I have yet several questions to ask him. Then they shall drag him to the gallows on a cowhide, and the hangman shall do his office a second time.

PHYSICIAN. (*steps up to the bed where courtiers and trabants are standing. They make room for him.*)

(*Gervasy and Protasy enter noiselessly, steal up to the king, writhing in a deep obeisance, each holding a piece of paper in his hand.*)

KING. You come pat, in good time, always in good time, my honest fellows. —Now I am master in my own house.

(*Gervasy and Protasy on bent knees; they leave.*)

KING. (*scans the papers, puts them away in his belt, looks about him. The court in a semi-circle.*)
Zdislaw!

(*A grandee steps forward.*)

KING. Last night your son expressed himself before witnesses as follows: If it should so come about that this mysterious stranger were really of royal blood, and if this prince should aspire to the crown, then he would not draw his sword against him. These are traitorous Ifs and murderous Ands! A tower stands empty high up in the mountains, there we will give him time to repent of his words. Rise. Step back.

(*To the Starosta of Utarkow, to whom he beckons to approach*)

You spoke to your wife when you were alone with her: you said there were such inward congestions and tainted humours as produced unexpectedly a strangulation of the overburdened head. With this covert speech you were alluding to us, the head of this realm.

STAROSTA OF UTARKOW. I know nothing! No one could have heard this!

KING. Step over there, rebel. The guard will carry you off. —You shall all look at one another and not know which one is not yet betrayed. Bohuslaw!

(*An old courtier steps forward.*)

KING. Why do you tremble so when I beckon to you graciously?

(Softly)

Your two maiden nieces are very beautiful. We must, whether we will or no, make of their twofold beauty the jewel of these approaching festive days.

(Louder)

Our good people will surely not wish to go without offering a pleasure-penny.

(To the chancellor)

See to it that the tax lists will be newly drawn up. From the Jewish quarter we expect a voluntary gift, worthy of such an occasion.

(Again to the old courtier)

The beauty of your nieces is exquisite.

(To the Castellan of Krakow)

Cover the gallows with black cloth. And also the statue of the most Blessed Virgin, opposite the scaffold, envelop it in black tissue. —But he shall wear a blood red shirt of scarlet, for he who has raised his hand against the sacred majesty ought to be regarded as a parricide—is it not so,

(turning to the confessor)

my father?

(To the old courtier)

Bring us the two maidens tonight, and be yourself the guardian of their honor. Make all arrangements, take to yourself the keys of our hunting lodge, be our master of the ceremonies. Go! go!

(*He grasps his hand before the old man can kiss the king's hand; he dismisses him, then turns suddenly to Count Adam.*)

Adam. We are greatly indebted to you for your presence of mind. Only do not run up your merits so high that we might become uneasy about being able to repay worthily. Favor that is stretched too far may easily shift about into disfavor. God forbid! Follow me, my courtiers. We will yet today give chase to a warrantable stag.

(*He walks with firm steps through the door on the right; the court follows him.*)

Physician. (*in the alcove*) Bandages on his feet. This light cloth over his face—O rare creature, precious like a single gem, you must not suffer disgrace!

Anton. (*comes running*) If you please, sir, come this way; my lord is in a worse state.

Julian. (*lies stretched on the ground, his head leaning against a chair, breathing with difficulty.*)

Physician. (*goes there, hands him a small bottle from his pocket*) Drink from this, sir, it will give you strength enough to take my arm and walk as far as my room where I shall bleed you.

(*To the guards who want to seize Julian, holding them off*)

Away with you! Here I command! I am responsible to his majesty and to no one else.

(*Softly to Julian who with Anton's help has raised himself to his feet*)

Now more than ever this noble youth entrusted to you is entitled to all your strength.

(*The servants, under the supervision of the doctor's assistant, have lifted Sigismund from the bed and carry him slowly out.*)

JULIAN. What do you want of me? What hope is yet left?
PHYSICIAN. The greatest. For he lives and will live, I promise
you. —Such and no other

(*he points to him who is being carried out*)

has ever been the narrow bed vouchsafed the saint for his
awakening.
JULIAN. And the hangman's clenched fist above the head! Already they are hammering at the scaffold!
PHYSICIAN. (*leads him one more step towards the front; in
a low voice*)
Acheronta movebo. I shall unbar the portals of hell and
make of the powers below my instrument: since the day
you were born this sentence had been written on the tablet
of your soul.

(*They walk slowly towards the door where the guards
have been posted.*)

JULIAN. How shall I understand you? You know, then—?
PHYSICIAN. (*stopping*) Violent is the time which endeavors
to renew itself through a chosen being. It will break chains
like straw, it will blow away granite walls like dust. That
I know.
JULIAN. Yes! Powerful man! How bright with knowledge
your eye shines. Stay with me. United with you—
PHYSICIAN. To set the forces free is our part, a higher power
decides the end. —We must be gone from here!

(*They go; the guards follow.*)

CURTAIN

ACT IV

(*A hall in the castle. On the left side wall a raised throne
under a canopy, next to it a concealed door. On the op-*

posite wall, a double door which leads out on a balcony. On the right front and in the center of the rear wall the main doors of the hall. Several old courtiers and several ladies. Pages and footmen, serving refreshments. Part of the company on the balcony, part inside. The passing bell rings persistently.)

FIRST OLD COURTIER. *(emptying his cup)* Is he still being led past the stands? It seems endless.

SECOND OLD COURTIER. *(looks down)* Now the priest is on the scaffold. High up there. A Paulist.

THIRD OLD COURTIER. *(coming in from the balcony)* A fan for the countess; the sun is on her face.

FIRST OLD COURTIER. A fan for the Countess Palatine. Bring one, pages.

SECOND OLD COURTIER. And his majesty on the platform, with the sun in his face; it has been two full hours by the clock!

FIRST OLD COURTIER. The sun is soon going down behind the roof of Sancta Maria.

SECOND OLD COURTIER. Thank God.

(On the balcony, restless strained attention. A page with a fan goes outside. The three old courtiers also step outside. Count Adam and the Starosta of Utarkow have entered through the door, next to the throne, which is concealed behind an arras. Both are very pale. They notice the people on the balcony and do not make a sound. The passing bell tinkles monotonously.)

ADAM. What does it feel like, Starosta, to witness an execution on the very day your own was fixed for?

STAROSTA. My nerves are too strained to answer witty questions. Why don't they fire the signal shot? Something has gone wrong.

ADAM. They will fire the shot as soon as the bell has stopped tolling. In the same instant the two thousand convicts fling themselves upon the horseguards.

STAROSTA. Why is the shot not fired? A plot which has five thousand accessories is lost over a minute's delay.

ADAM. The shot will be fired as soon as the bell stops tinkling.

STAROSTA. It is not possible, he must long since have gone up the steps to the gallows. Something is wrong. We are betrayed, Adam!

(*Puts his hand to his sword*)

Basilius shall not have me alive.

(*The bell is silent. They listen tensely.*)

ADAM. Quiet, Starosta. Now we play the great play. In three seconds we strike the king, or the king strikes us.

(*A shot is heard down below, directly followed by more. Shouting. Commotion on the balcony. A few ladies jump to their feet. A shriek.*)

ADAM. We strike the king! Quick, Starosta, to your post.

(*The Starosta lifts the arras and disappears. Count Adam runs to the rear door, opens it and disappears. All the ladies come in from the balcony.*)

THE LADIES. What is it? What has happened!

ONE LADY. They are pulling the dragoons from their horses!

YOUNG LADY. I saw the bannerets around the king draw their sabers! What does that mean?

AN OLD COURTIER. Insurrection! It is high treason, a conspiracy!

SECOND OLD COURTIER. Then why don't the guards fire?

(*One alarm bell begins ringing, then several. Everyone in the hall running about in confusion.*)

FIRST LADY. You cannot make it out clearly. They are shouting something.

SECOND LADY. I am afraid.

SECOND OLD COURTIER. Why don't the guards fire? Help for the king!

(*He draws.*)

(*Ladies run toward the door at the right front and come back directly.*)

(*The Steward of the Table runs to the concealed door on the left.*)

OLD COURTIER. You there, where to?
STEWARD. To secure the gold plate. The world's upside down.

(*Disappears through the small door.*)

THE LADIES. The main staircase is cut off. No one is allowed through! —How, cut off? By the troops?
OLD LADY. We must get out. Who commands the guard?
YOUNG LADY. This way! Through the chapel!

(*They try to leave by the door at the back.*)

COUNT ADAM. (*with an officer of the guard enters the hall through the door at the back*)
No one leaves here. Take everyone here present into custody.
YOUNG LADY. What has happened?
COUNT ADAM. The ladies that way, please. Through the chapel. The staircase will be shut off. The king is coming directly up here.

(*Below, shouting. Several shots.*)

OLD COURTIER. Our king is below there in the hands of rebels.
COUNT ADAM. (*turning back*) Post the guard!

(*To those in front*)

His majesty, King Sigismund, will be here immediately in the midst of his trusted bannerets.

(*To the guard*)

Long live the King!
GUARD. *Vivat* Sigismund!
THE LADIES. (*leave the hall past the guards.*)
THE OLD COURTIERS. High treason!

(*They draw.*)

COUNT ADAM. (*very calmly*) Disarm them! Take them away!
THE OLD COURTIERS. (*are led away.*)

(*Count Adam and the officer follow them. The door is
closed at once. The concealed door opens. Gervasy and
Protasy come out, peering anxiously.*)

GERVASY. (*at the door in the back, listens.*)
PROTASY. (*sneaks toward the window to peer down, then to
the door at the right.*)

(*Basilius' face looks out behind the arras.*)

PROTASY. (*softly to Gervasy*) Locked?
GERVASY. The room is full of men; they are holding their
breath, but their weapons are clanking.
PROTASY. (*noiselessly goes up to him*) There is an eye at the
key hole. They are looking in.
GERVASY. (*tries to look through the key hole*) Here too.

(*Basilius steps forward, in a magnificent but damaged
cloak, the naked sword in his hand. No one is with him
except an old courtier.*)

PROTASY AND GERVASY. (*signal to him, warning him.*)
BASILIUS. How did I escape them?
THE OLD COURTIER. They did not dare lay their hands on
the anointed king.
BASILIUS. (*pale with anger*) Not one shall escape with his
life. Why do my guards not fire? Call the officer who
commands the palace guard. Bring him to me right here.

(*Gervasy and Protasy come closer, their hand on their mouths.*)

THE OLD COURTIER. Back, my gracious lord! Back! through the chapel. You are lost here.

(*He lifts the arras. Basilius leaves, the courtier behind him.*)

(*Gervasy wants to follow, Protasy behind.*)

GERVASY. (*recoils*) The door won't open. It is bolted from outside. Now they have him.

(*They listen.*)

PROTASY. They have caught him in the mouse trap.
GERVASY. And us with him.

(*Outside a fanfare.*)

(*Gervasy and Protasy hide behind an arras. The double doors behind them open.*)

COUNT ADAM. (*steps in; guards are visible behind him.*)

(*Another fanfare.*)

SIGISMUND. (*enters from the right, half led, half carried by the Vaivodes. He wears a long white shirt; over it, tattered remnants of the scarlet robe. Two of them conduct Sigismund to the throne. The guard offer a military salute. Outside, fanfares.*)

(*All the Vaivodes kneel in front of the throne. Sigismund gives a faint sign to rise.*)

PALATINE OF KRAKOW. (*remains kneeling*) With raised hands we beg your forgiveness that we could not spare your exalted person this procession across the market place. We needed the revolt of the lowest classes in order to sweep along all and to overwhelm the troop.
SIGISMUND. I pray you, rise, gentlemen.

(Somewhat stronger)

I wish to see no one kneel! —I should have been kneeling this minute to lay my head upon the block.

PALATINE OF KRAKOW. *(kneeling)* Even now, before the crown has been lowered on your majesty's head, the golden glory of a saint and martyr encircles it for all time to come.

(He rises. All the others with him. They stand facing Sigismund. The Vaivode of Lublin and the Chancellor of Lithuania approach Sigismund who sits; they remain standing on the lowest step on both sides of the throne.)

VAIVODE OF LUBLIN. Is your highness able now to grant us your attention?

CHANCELLOR. *(calling toward the back)* The physician! His highness needs a tonic!

PALATINE OF KRAKOW. *(calling to the back)* Chamberlains! Provide us clothes for his majesty.

ANTON. *(at the door in the back, to the soldiers lined up on both sides)* Let me in, I must go to my master.

(He is let through.)

SIGISMUND. *(looks at Anton who is coming closer)* Anton!

ANTON. Is my master not here?

(Looks about him, frightened)

Your Highness! Your Majesty! Where is his lordship, my gracious master?

SIGISMUND. *(says something that is inaudible.)*

(Vaivode of Lublin and Chancellor of Lithuania step up closer to him.)

SIGISMUND. Find him! My teacher!

CHANCELLOR. Whom does your highness wish to be found?

SIGISMUND. The one who was imprisoned with me! The one they dragged on the cowhide.

ANTON. Shall I go?

SIGISMUND. (*nods to him.*)

VAIVODE OF LUBLIN. The count is uninjured, I can answer for it. He was informed about everything. He will be brought here later. But now your highness needs all your strength for the state affairs that cannot be postponed.

(*Commotion at the door in front. Calls from among the Vaivodes: "The clerks, let the clerks through! No one else!"*)

CHANCELLOR. (*goes to the door, lets two public scribes enter*) From now on no one enters here who is not a banneret.

VAIVODE OF LUBLIN. (*calls over the heads of the guards*) Push them down the stairs, the gentry. The country delegates into the courtyard. Close it off!

PALATINE. The Supreme Court of Law is now in session, and no one is to come into this hall.

OFFICER. Guard, about face!

(*The guard turns, facing outward.*)

SIGISMUND. Let some go and bring the one they dragged on the cowhide.

ANTON. (*tears the scarlet shreds off Sigismund*) Some of them have gone, Your Majesty!

SEVERAL. Bring in Basilius. There is no time to be lost!

CHANCELLOR. Captain of the guard!

OFFICER. (*steps forward.*)

CHANCELLOR. You are commissioned, sir, with six officers to seize the person of the former king in the Carabiniers' Hall and to present him here.

OFFICER. At once, Your Grace.

SIGISMUND. (*whispers meanwhile to Anton.*)

ANTON. (*goes to the line of soldiers in the back*) I must get clothes for the king.

(*They let him through.*)

SIGISMUND. (*about to descend from the throne*) I wish to go
with him and find the one whom they dragged on the
cowhide.

(*The Vaivode of Lublin and the Chancellor of Lithuania
gently urge him back on the throne.*)

VAIVODE OF LUBLIN. We beg you humbly to submit. A most
important act of state demands of your highness self-
possession and presence of mind.

CHANCELLOR. It is necessary, my gracious Lord! It is necessary.

(*Drumbeat, slow, muffled, on the outside. The guard clears
the door at the right front, and forms in line for the procession coming in. The courtiers step back and make room.*)

BASILIUS. (*bareheaded, without weapons, in a magnificent
but damaged cloak, between the halberds of two bodyguards. Four more behind, the officer with drawn sword
in front.*)

OFFICER. (*salutes with the sword.*)

CHANCELLOR. (*signals him to step aside with the guards, then
takes a scroll from the hand of one clerk*)
Basilius, you have been called before us to read in a loud
voice the manifesto of your abdication and to sign it before
all our eyes.

BASILIUS. My abdication is to be deliberated here? —I demand legal counsel for the crown. Who represents my
rights here? What kind of court is this?

SEVERAL VOICES. (*very sharply*) Enough!

CHANCELLOR. (*handing him the document, in a low but em-
phatic voice*) Read and sign it!

BASILIUS. (*unfolds the document and looks in, then*)
I have come here after I was given solemn assurance of my

life in the other hall. Where are the courtiers? Why did
they not accompany me?

VAIVODE OF LUBLIN. Read out the manifesto; there is nothing
to discuss!

BASILIUS. (*looks at Sigismund who does not seem to take
notice of him, unfolds the document and reads*)
"I, Basilius, heretofore King of Poland . . ." The rest of
the titles are missing here!

CHANCELLOR. They will be inserted later. Make haste!

BASILIUS. (*reads*) ". . . King of Poland, at the height of my
sins illuminated by God's punishing bolt of lightning, have
recognized my unworthiness, and thrown from the summit
of my pride, have sought the advice of my ever loyal and
true cousins, the Vaivodes, Palatines, and bannerets—"

VAIVODE OF LUBLIN. Bow down at this point!

BASILIUS. (*looks at him, then makes an exaggerated bow, and
continues reading*) "—to which I submit, absolutely and
without complaint."

(*He sighs.*)

PALATINE OF KRAKOW. Continue!

BASILIUS. (*reads*) "Recognized as a tyrant and thief, traitor
to the land and my own crown"—recognized, how? —Oh,
recognized by you!—

SEVERAL VOICES. Continue!

BASILIUS. (*reads*) "—I resign this crown, relinquish the seal,
lay down the War Lord's staff and the standard"—the
standard also?— "—waive my prerogatives and dignities,
renounce my rank"—that? How so? That I cannot!

VAIVODE OF LUBLIN. Stand still, Basilius!

VOICES. Finish it! Let the Chancellor read!

PALATINE OF KRAKOW. (*standing in front, to the chancellor*)
If it please your Grace to read the document aloud to the
end so that we may come to the signature!

CHANCELLOR. (*takes the document from Basilius' hand and*

217

reads) "—renounce my rank and shall be from this hour no longer King and Lord over the lands of the Polish crown, but the most culpable subject of the aforesaid crown and await, submitting to such custody as will be appointed—"

BASILIUS. But my life is assured! Will it say so anywhere in this paper?

CHANCELLOR. (*with raised voice*) "—await the decrees which the Council of State in its wisdom will adopt."

BASILIUS. More decrees? But not concerning me! I shall retire with a small household to a manor house which will be assigned to me.

CHANCELLOR. (*raising his voice*) "Issued in my royal castle of former times, on the last day—"

BASILIUS. The last? How, the last? This could be misinterpreted!—

CHANCELLOR. "—on the last day of my abode therein, under the seal of my successor, upon whom may descend the blessing of the Almighty."

BASILIUS. Not, of my son? Your Highness' reversion is still in abeyance?

(*He bows exaggeratedly around the circle, but not to Sigismund.*)

May God bless your collective majesty!

CHANCELLOR. Hand him a pen.

CLERK. (*does so.*)

BASILIUS. (*looks in the document*) That is all? Such few words? So plain?

(*He takes the pen mechanically from the hand of the clerk.*)

The most important point is left out. The sum for my maintenance is not named. There is no table.

VAIVODE OF LUBLIN. (*points to the lowest step in front of the throne.*)

BASILIUS. The king beckons to me. He seems to want to speak with me.

VAIVODE OF LUBLIN. Here, sign!

BASILIUS. (*kneels down and signs; then he rises and speaks to Sigismund*)

Son, you have made of me a poor, helpless earthworm—I am going.

(*To the courtiers*)

My life and my maintenance are assured to me!

(*Again turning around to Sigismund*)

Our cousins are cleverer at overthrowing than at supporting kings. I warn your highness.

VAIVODE OF LUBLIN. Silence, Basilius. Bow before his highness and these gentlemen, your judges, and retire.

(*To the officer who steps forward*)

Escort him there.

BASILIUS. There? Does that mean: to the tower? I will not let myself be taken there! I have never sent an old man to that tower. A child can be alone—an old man cannot be alone. Let me go!

(*He leaps to the side.*)

I have not committed a crime deserving death. I did not kill him. It rested with me yet in the last moment to grant his pardon. Who can know whether I was not determined to wave the white kerchief!

CHANCELLOR. Trabants! Put an end to this!

TRABANTS. (*stand undecided, look at their officer.*)

BASILIUS. Wait! I could be taken to a monastery. That is permissible. I have clerical prerogatives. The king is the supreme pastor of souls. Bring the cardinal; he is responsible for my soul! I want no court about me, but give me books

I can devote myself to—I want edifying books—plainly printed—

OFFICER. Take him, trabants!

BASILIUS. (*runs from them, holds on to one leg of the throne*) —plainly printed with intelligible pictures, for my heart is still the heart of a child—only the world has corrupted me. I appeal! I hold you accountable!

TRABANTS. (*have taken hold of him and brought him to his feet.*)

BASILIUS. You will witness an edifying miracle if I am treated gently—but if I am locked in a solitary tower, you will have a desperate person on your hands!

TRABANTS. (*take him away.*)

(*It has grown half dark. At the back door servants enter with candelabra, others, among them Anton, with clothing and a cloak; the physician in front.*)

ANTON. The clothes for the king, captain, sir!

(*The line of soldiers lets them pass.*)

VAIVODE OF LUBLIN. Before in fealty on our knees we salute your highness as our Majesty and Lord, you will take an oath with hand and lips upon the Constitutum which

(*he beckons to the second clerk*)

I here hold in my hands.

SIGISMUND. (*recognizes Julian who has entered, muffled in disguise, among the servants; he rises.*)

PALATINE OF KRAKOW. Is your majesty giving us your attention? It is necessary.

SIGISMUND. May my household servants come to me? You gentlemen are fully dressed, and I am wearing only a shirt.

(*He goes down the steps. The servants approach him, also those carrying the candles, and conceal Sigismund from view. Shots are heard in the distance. Several of the Vaivodes look out of the balcony door.*)

FIRST SERVANT. Shooting in the outskirts of the town. There's no help for it—the rabble that has been let loose must be put back on the chain again, and with bloody force.

SECOND SERVANT. The devil sows his seeds between the grain; that's the way it goes.

SIGISMUND. (*steps forward.*)

JULIAN. (*next to him.*)

SIGISMUND. (*softly to him*) Stay close to me now, my teacher.

CHANCELLOR. (*steps before Sigismund*) It appears necessary that the several powers of the Council of State be fixed by a solemn constitution. The point being that your highness will be bound by oath—

SIGISMUND. (*holds his hand out to the physician who kisses it. Then he seats himself on the throne.*)

VAIVODE. If it please your highness to grant the chancellor audience. It is essential. This fundamental act of state for which we are assembled here should not be delayed.

SIGISMUND. (*steps down, goes up to the Vaivodes*)
Down there I was carried past all of you—I saw your face —yours—yours! You hid your face in your hands. You looked at me firmly and I understood that you wished to give me comfort. You gave me a sign pointing up to heaven.

(*They bow reverently and kiss his hand.*)

But now go, my cousins, and leave me alone with this man,

(*he points to Julian*)

for he will be my minister, and I wish to take counsel with him.

VAIVODE OF LUBLIN. (*goes up to Julian with vigorous steps*)
Count Julian, be gone from this hall which no one has authorized you to enter.

PALATINE OF KRAKOW. The constitution contains the names

of those noble persons with whom alone the king may take counsel.

CHANCELLOR. The royal seal remains to hand, jointly of the Council and the King.

JULIAN. The seal is in my hands. In the king's name: my lords, you are given leave to depart. When there is need of your counsel, we shall know how to find you.

THE VAIVODES. (*menacing*) We shall know how to find you! We shall know how to strike! We shall know how to punish!

JULIAN. Officer! In the name of the king. These gentlemen will leave us. Clear the doorway for them.

THE VAIVODES. (*put their hands to their swords*) Oho! We shall see about that.

JULIAN. (*very strong*) Guards! Who is king in Poland?

OFFICER. (*takes his stand somewhat near Sigismund*) Standard to me!

STANDARD-BEARER. (*steps behind the officer. Fanfare outside.*)

GUARDS. (*holding their pikes crosswise, move between Sigismund and the Vaivodes so that they must yield one step.*)

JULIAN. Your lordships are cleverer at unseating a king than at setting him on the throne; you shall be treated accordingly.

GUARDS. (*holding their pikes crosswise, take one step forward; the Vaivodes take one step back towards the exit.*)

PALATINE OF KRAKOW. A royal decree without our consent is null and void!

THE VAIVODES. That is so!

GUARDS. (*take a step forward.*)

JULIAN. We shall know how to preserve the royal seal from misuse.

VAIVODE OF LUBLIN. Traitor, you stole the seals! That is a capital crime!

GUARDS. (*take one step forward.*)

JULIAN. Retire, my lords, to your houses without delay!

Each by himself! Any banding together will be dealt with as high treason.

GUARDS. (*take one step forward.*)

THE VAIVODES (*already quite near the door, shake their fists*) We have not yet done with you!

JULIAN. To this end, your lordships, are kings empowered by God, that they create order out of disorder.

THE VAIVODES. (*are being forced out.*)

GUARDS. (*at both doors withdraw.*)

ANTON. (*pushes an armchair up for Sigismund, then for Julian.*)

PHYSICIAN. (*steps into the background.*)

JULIAN. (*steps in front of Sigismund, bending his knee, then rising at once*)

O my king! my son! —for you come from me who molded you, not from him who furnished merely the clump of earth, nor from her who gave birth to you, howling, before she departed this world! I have shaped you for this hour! Now do not let me down! —I understand your look. Your soul has had to suffer in order to rise—and all else was vain.

SIGISMUND. You have taught me to comprehend it. All is vain except the discourse between spirit and spirit. —But now I, the begotten son, am above the begetter. Now when I lie alone, my spirit goes out where yours does not reach.

JULIAN. Yes? Are you filled with a foreboding? a glorious foreboding of your Self? A prodigious future?

SIGISMUND. Future and present at one and the same time.

JULIAN. Exalted being, the royal mantle can raise you no higher. I have led you out of your tower, dressed you in princely robes, but what was that compared with the road which I have now opened before you!

SIGISMUND. (*smiling*) True! For now I shall never run the danger that the phantom will prove to be a phantom.

JULIAN. You speak true, my king. For this time you are secure.

SIGISMUND. Yes, that I am, Lord and King for ever in this solid tower.

(He strikes himself on his breast.)

JULIAN. We are now the fortune-tellers and the fortune-makers.

SIGISMUND. Yes, we are. Fortunate to have been taught by experience!

(He sits down.)

JULIAN. To do the deeds, that is henceforth our part.

SIGISMUND. That is our part.

JULIAN. And now to horse and ride with me where you will look upon legions of your loyal men as the moon on judgment day will look upon them that have risen, and her eye will not be large enough to encompass the multitude. —Hear me! Understand me right! My deeds, concealed from you, were fulfillment; a plan, a tremendous plan, underneath it all. Even on the cowhide I was stronger than all of them together. Do you hear me? These swaggering grandees were the hunting dogs. Now that the stag is down, you drive them off with the whip. An enormous uprising, unsuspected by them, moves this night with gaping jaws across the whole land like the bear climbing over the roof of a sheepfold. I have pushed on to the limit, the earth itself I have tickled to life and what dwells inside it, the peasant, the clod of earth, with his fearful strength—I have blown breath into his nostrils—his swinish snout and his wolfish maw utter your name, and with earthy hands he strangles the beadles and the bailiffs that obstruct his way. —In your name I have called up the *szlachta*—ten thousand of them, Polish gentry, will ride and take you into their midst; fifty thousand peasants are up and have forged their scythes into pikes.

(Opens the balcony door; the sky is flaming red.)

ANTON. The fire bells are ringing out from all the churches on the outskirts of the town, the wind brings with it a strong burning smell. And the heavy cannon can be heard. Now, what might that be?

A SERVANT. *(carrying a riding habit over his arm has entered from the left and stands waiting.)*

JULIAN. Living proof of what I have done. —That is my cannon and those who fire it are my men. The mines have yielded their living entrails; with burning stakes naked men advance on a square of muskets—the last judgment has come for all who have not understood the signs of the time. —The great lords stand now on their palace balconies and piss for fear. —Do you hear the shouts? There is no one who does not march this night and shout your name. —But I shall hold them together for you: I subdue force with force, the soldier with the peasant, the flat lands with the fortified towns, the great lords with a levy of the barons, and them with the Switzer regiments that I have put on oath for you, and thus the reins will remain in your hands. —There, take up, my king! Clothe yourself! We will ride out. Why do you look at me like that?

SIGISMUND. I understand what you will, but I will not.

JULIAN. You will not?

(Fails to understand this)

Ah, but yes! Quick! His riding habit! The belt!

SIGISMUND. I stand firm, and you cannot move me from this spot. I have nothing to do with your schemes.

PHYSICIAN. *(approaches Sigismund.)*

JULIAN. My king! Do not fail me now, for now or never your hour has come.

SIGISMUND. What do you know of me? Do you have access to me? who am inaccessible as if surrounded by a thousand trabants.

JULIAN. Just put on the dress! And buckle on your sword! Horses are ready! They must see you now. Then I will answer for the outcome.

SIGISMUND. Farewell, Julian.

(*He turns away.*)

JULIAN. My king! What are you doing to me?

SIGISMUND. You have put me in the straw like an apple, and I have become ripe, and now I know my place. But it is not where you would have me.

(*They look into one another's eyes.*)

PHYSICIAN. Consider, your excellency, what a day the king has lived through.

SIGISMUND. No, my friend. It is simply that I will not. But when I say: I will, then you shall see how gloriously I go out of this house.

ANTON. (*softly to Julian*) Let be, my lord. He's grown deep over the things they have done to him.

(*The door on the right opens a little. Simon shuffles in.*)

PHYSICIAN. A bedchamber has been made ready here below this hall. I shall watch with the servants.

JULIAN. (*notices Simon, goes up to him.*) How did you come in? How did the guard let you pass?

SIMON. There are no guards anywhere. Not a soul in the anteroom. Not a soul on the stairs.

SIGISMUND. I shall sleep. Much will happen tomorrow, and then I must not stand aside. Farewell, Julian.

(*He goes; Anton goes before him, opens the door at the back; the physician follows him.*)

JULIAN. You come from the suburbs, on the other side?

SIMON. It was easy to get there, but coming back was difficult enough.

JULIAN. I see a strong glare of fire. But the shooting has stopped.

SIMON. They that have property have crept into a mouse-hole. The common rabble is hopping and dancing. Who is there to shoot at?

JULIAN. The Switzers hold the bridge from the outskirts?

SIMON. The Switzers are gone.

JULIAN. Gone?

SIMON. By order of the Council, they say.

JULIAN. (*calls*) Jerzy!

GROOM. (*enters from the right with Julian's hat and sword.*)

JULIAN. (*to the groom*) My horses are below by the castle guard?

GROOM. The horses are down below—but there's no guard any more. They've all quietly left.

JULIAN. The castle guard left?

SIMON. That is the whole point. They have changed the watchword. In fact, everything is completely changed. Not a word about our new king, his highness. No mention of your excellency. The one without a name, he is now in complete power over there.

JULIAN. The nameless one is called Olivier and acts on my command.

GROOM. (*steps nearer.*)

SIMON. Very good. He is in power now. He has the artillery and the men. But it does not look as if he were one to take commands.

GROOM. Your excellency did send an officer to him: he should stop his shooting and burning. That is what he charged him with. And he answered: he was just beginning. And as for his coming here and reporting to you, he would come in time, but with twenty thousand behind him. And without more ado shoots the officer down from his horse. His groom escaped and has reported it.

JULIAN. Before dawn the levy of nobles will be to their rear. Where are the squadrons now? Is it known?

SIMON. The gentlemen are all gone into the great forests—
over there. But they don't come out.

JULIAN. How? They don't come out?

SIMON. Their feet are up in the air. —The rebels have over-
run them and hung them all from the trees.

JULIAN. I have opened the gates of hell, and now all hell has
broken loose. Then I must look it in the face.

(*Buckles on his sword, puts his hat on, and goes out rapidly.*)

GROOM. (*follows him. Simon sneaks out.*)

CURTAIN

ACT V

(*An antechamber in the castle; on the right an iron grating, with a door inside it leading to a further antechamber.
On the left, two doors. It is nighttime, close to morning.
On the left wall not far from the second door is a low
bedstead.*)

ANTON. (*dressed, cowers on the bed; he rises, goes to the
grating, and peeks through.*)
Officer! Sir!
Are you there? Nobody there? Nobody at all?

(*He takes a tinderbox, kindles a light, and holds it through
the grating.*)

Where are the guards? Where is the sentinel? Doctor!
This is sickening—I am scared!

(*Goes to the nearer door on the left*)

Can you hear me, doctor?

PHYSICIAN. (*comes out*) What is it, Anton?

ANTON. The sentinel is gone—there's nobody left. What is going on, doctor?

PHYSICIAN. Is the king asleep?

(*Listens at the farther door.*)

ANTON. (*in the background at the window*) Some people are running down there with lanterns. They are bringing some one! I don't like it at all.

JULIAN'S GROOM. (*appears at the grating*) Disaster! My lord is dead!

PHYSICIAN. (*runs to him*) Quiet, don't shout—the king is asleep.

GROOM. Shot him down from his horse. Stabbed him with pikes as he lay on the ground. They are bringing him.

ANTON. Who is bringing him?

GROOM. Our men. But ours are not alone. With them such bareheaded, barefoot rabble.

SIGISMUND. (*steps softly out of his door; they do not notice him.*)

ANTON. Now it's life or death. Holy Mother of Jesus!

PHYSICIAN. (*exits with the groom through the door behind the grating.*)

SIGISMUND. Why does Anton clench his fists?

ANTON. Quick, hide yourself! They shoot at anything that smacks of lordship.

SIGISMUND. (*steps calmly to the window, looks down.*)

ANTON. (*tripping with fright*) If only these things did not happen so fast! For twenty years it all went along so slowly!

(*Men are approaching on the right, outside the grating. Torch light.*)

ANTON. Now it's coming: hand round the throat, the knee on the chest! —How did I ever come into this confounded country. I can't keep my wits straight any more!

VOICES. (*very close*) Sigismund! Sigismund!

ANTON. Now these hot devils bellow your name! Hide yourself, for the love of—hide yourself inside!

SIGISMUND. Here I am. Go and meet them, point to me and
shout loudly: Here he stands, the man you are looking for.
Then they will not harm you.

(*The physician, the groom and Anton carry in Julian. His
eyes are closed and he looks like a dead man. At the same
time rebels enter the room, partly armed, partly unarmed.
Among them are several with stern faces and long hair,
holding torches in their hands; some are half naked, still
wearing severed chains around their feet and iron rings
around the neck. Most of them stay outside and look in
through the iron grating. Julian is placed on the low bedstead which Anton had occupied before.*)

ONE IN FRONT. Look on him, naked brethren! first born sons
of Adam! Behold: the king's son underneath the earth,
chained to the streaming vaults! This is the one!

ONE WITH A WOODEN LEG. (*pushes his way forward*) This one
is the poor man's king, and they will carry before him the
sword and the scales.

SIGISMUND. (*looks motionless on Julian.*)

ANTON. (*softly to the physician*) Must our master die?

ONE OF THEM. Speak to us!

ANOTHER. Call him by his name!

A THIRD. Those that have called him by name, their tongue
has grown dumb in their mouths.

JULIAN. (*opens his eyes, raises himself partly and looks about.
Two with torches stand near his bed.*)
Where am I?

(*He looks around in a circle, with difficulty.*)

You—face of a rat! You—front of a swine with eyes that
squint upwards! You snout of a dog! Clods, all of you,
shuffling about! By the light of this torch, I will laugh at
you without being tickled!

(He raises himself completely.)

Take your pikes away!

(They make room.)

Ha, Nothingness growing a thousand heads, stand up beneath my look. As long as I subdue you with my eyes I shall not be deprived of the sense of my self!

ONE WITH A TORCH. The flock has no shepherd. But they who hold staffs and swords in their hands are devils. We make short shrift of them. So you are condemned.

JULIAN. You have condemned me? You are the sweepings that I have alone swept together!

SIGISMUND. *(takes one step nearer to Julian)*
My teacher, why do you speak to them? The tongue is too thick to say what is worth the trouble of saying.

JULIAN. *(turns toward him)*
You are also here, creature of mine? —He is, as he stands there, my work and it is wretched.

THE ONE WITH THE TORCH. We are the light-bearers, the anabaptists in the fire. You are our light, and now we will choke the prince of darkness with our naked hands.

ONE IN RAGS. We stand at your side! Speak to us, our king!

SIGISMUND. *(nearer to Julian)* My teacher, I am near you.

JULIAN. Turn away from me, you lump of clay, under whose tongue I have put the wrong word. I do not wish to see you.

SIGISMUND. You have put the right word under my tongue, the word of comfort in the desert of this life—and I give it you again in this hour.

JULIAN. *(lies down again; he shuts his eyes.)*

SIGISMUND. I smile to you in your solitude. —Your prayer is not without virtue even though you clench your fists instead of folding your hands.

JULIAN. *(opens his eyes and closes them again)*

I have brought the lowest up above. But it has not borne fruit.

SIGISMUND. You torment yourself that a vein may break open inside you from which you might drink. But inside me it flows without hindrance, and that is your work.

JULIAN. (*opens his eyes once more as if he were about to speak; then he shuts his eyes and sinks back with one word.*)

Nothing!

SIGISMUND. (*looks at him*) He is dead.

THE ONE WITH THE TORCH. Do not heed the dead man; for you will remain with us forever.

AN OLD MAN. (*makes his way forward*)

Look on him, on our king, how he stands here. Like one bathed in the living waters of the river, he gleams from head to foot.

ONE OF THEM. Speak to us!

ANOTHER. Do not wake him. If he were to cry out, our soul would burst in us like a sack.

ONE ALMOST NAKED. (*with a chain on his foot*) We know you well. You were carried past us, you Lamb of God, and to each one of us you gave greeting with your dying eyes!

(*He bends down and kisses Sigismund's garment.*)

ANOTHER. Remain with us! endure with us!

SIGISMUND. (*in an undertone, as if to himself*) Yes, I will go out with you.

ONE OF THEM. He speaks to us. He says he will go out with us.

ANOTHER. (*kneeling down*) That we may not die, O lord!

ONE OF THEM. Form a lane so that all who stand outside can see him.

SIGISMUND. I feel a broad open land. It smells of earth and salt. I will go there.

ONE OF THEM. We will fit out a cart and yoke twelve pair

of oxen to it. You shall ride on it before us, and a bell shall ring on your cart as if you were a church riding on wheels.

VOICES. (*inside and outside*) Remain with us! endure with us!

ONE OF THE NAKED. (*with an iron ring around his neck*) We are uncovered—but may we clothe you? Will our king consent that we clothe him with a robe of gold?

ANOTHER. We took it down from the altar and we would put it on you with reverence.

SIGISMUND. (*views the naked figures*) These are untrimmed people. We will live together under the sky; I dislike those who live in houses.

THE ONE WITH THE TORCH. Therefore we shall not leave one stone upon another in the churches; for God does not hide himself in a house.

SEVERAL. Let us lift you and carry you out that all may see you.

OTHERS. (*further back*) Lord, protect us! Endure with us!

(*They sigh.*)

(*A sharp roll of drums outside, quite near by.*)

SIGISMUND. (*starts in alarm.*)

THE ONE WITH THE TORCH. Fear not, for you are a torch, and no one can extinguish you.

SIGISMUND. Who is this who now wants to come to me? I hear his footsteps on the stairs.

ANOTHER OF THE TORCH-BEARERS. The hairs on your head are numbered, and there is no one who would lift his hand against you.

SIGISMUND. (*very anxious*) But who are they that are coming now?

ONE OF THE NAKED. They are those without a name who until now have commanded us. But we set you above them. Come then on our shoulders and speak to them from above.

233

SIGISMUND. No, there is someone coming now whom I must face.

(*A short drum roll outside.*)

OLIVIER. (*steps in, covered with iron and leather, pistols in his belt, a battle helmet on his head, a short iron club in his hand. Behind him Jeronim, the scribe, and the Latvian Indrik; they too are armed with short pikes.*)

(*The people make room.*)

OLIVIER. (*steps up to Sigismund, contemplates him.*)

ONE OF THE PEOPLE. This is the chosen one! He shall ride before us on a cart with bells.

ANOTHER. All that has happened has happened for his sake.

A THIRD ONE. At his feet all will kiss one another, and the wolf will embrace the lamb. Therefore he must ride before us on a cart.

OLIVIER. Good. It shall be so ordered.

(*He notices Julian's dead body, approaches it; the people make room.*)

I know him. He was your jailer. He kept you worse than a dog, and now he is repaid.

SIGISMUND. You are mistaken. He did not keep me as he was commanded to, but he kept me as he had planned in the fulfillment of his mind's work.

OLIVIER. Get rid of the dead Jesuit.

SIGISMUND. No, carry him in there and lay him on my bed.

(*Several men raise Julian up and carry him into the next room.*)

THE ONE WITH THE TORCH. (*going up to Sigismund*) We are always at your side! We will stay around this house to answer your call.

OLIVIER. Off with you, make room.

A SECOND ONE WITH A TORCH. (*turning to Olivier*) We know no ruling power. Should you nameless ones try to set yourselves up—you will be condemned.

OLIVIER. You are deceived! There is no governing power—but there are those whom you charged with doing what must be done. —Now leave me alone with this person.

(*Aron, Jeronim, and Indrik hold their pikes crosswise and force the people out of the hall. Drum roll outside. The people give way silently, all eyes on Sigismund.*)

SIGISMUND. (*points to Anton*) This one shall remain with me. Anton, I am thirsty. Bring me something to drink, Anton.

PHYSICIAN. (*is one of the last to leave the room; not with the others, but alone by the door at the front, right.*)

ANTON. (*places a candlestick on the table.*)

OLIVIER. (*in an undertone to his three followers*) You will stay within calling distance, my adjutants, all three of you.

(*To Aron still more softly*)

Those incendiaries with the torches, isolate them in the courtyard. Have them surrounded with reliable people; attract no attention.

(*Aron, Jeronim, and Indrik go off.*)

OLIVIER. I have to speak with you, and you will answer me.

SIGISMUND. (*looks at him, looks away again.*)

OLIVIER. Do you know before whom you are standing?

SIGISMUND. (*remains silent.*)

OLIVIER. We are your helpers. We snatched you from under the axe when it whistled through the air.

SIGISMUND. Yes, they had already disposed of my head, removed it to some other place. But thereby, as when one places an iron finger under the hinge, they have lifted out a door in front of me, and I have stepped behind a wall where I can hear all that you speak, but none of you can come to me, and I am safe from your hands.

(*He sits down.*)

Anton, look outside, where are those with whom I had made friends just now? Is the doctor also with them?

ANTON. Better mind this man here; his word counts for a great deal now.

OLIVIER. Sigismund! The time has come to make amends for what you have suffered. You shall have an important office.

ANTON. (*in a low voice*) Thank him kindly.

OLIVIER. As we start on our march now, you will ride on a cart and they will come by the thousands and hail you, because you have driven your father from the throne. In this way the ignorant, tongue-tied people will be taught by us to read emblems with their eyes, and the lords will plunge head over heels into the earth. But you will be well content; instead of an earthen jug you will have full silver bowls to swill from, and women will take you to your bath and wait upon you.

SIGISMUND. (*to Anton*) Let all those that are friendly to me hold together and come for me.

ANTON. Heed this man; he has great power.

OLIVIER. You do not answer me? You are a sly rogue, son of Basilius. You've smelled it: now is the time to exercise power; you would have power then and not the mere show of it. You are right! We shall draw the shrewd men to us, but the stupid ones we shall ride. Come now, and we will see of what use you can be among those that command.

SIGISMUND. (*with contempt*) Who is it that gave you power to hand out to others?

OLIVIER. Do you see this iron tool in my hand? The hand grips it and strikes with it; just so I am myself in the hand of fatality. What you are facing now you have never known before. What you have known up to now was jesuitical machinations and hocus-pocus. But now you are face to face with reality.

SIGISMUND. I understand you well. I know that the Here and Now fetters many men as with a chain. But not me, for I am here and I am not here! So you may not command me.

OLIVIER. That is what I have you for, you and your kind, in order to put you to good use.

SIGISMUND. You do not have me. For I am alone unto myself. You do not even see me: for you are incapable of looking, because you eyes are walled up with that which is not.

OLIVIER. Is that all you have to answer me? Epileptic creature, can you not see who stands before you?

SIGISMUND. I see you have the neck of an ox and the eyes of a dog. So you are fit for the task that has been set you.

OLIVIER. That is all?

ANTON. (*afraid, folds his hands.*)

SIGISMUND. I have always had people like you sitting about me in my pigsty.

(*He gets up, turns his back on Olivier, and goes slowly out of the back door, on the left. Anton follows him.*)

OLIVIER. (*tosses his head three times in a dreadful threat*) It is enough. It is enough. It is enough.—
Come in, adjutants, all three!

(*Aron, Jeronim, Indrik enter.*)

OLIVIER. Have you done away with Basilius?

JERONIM. We have. On the stroke of seven. Against a cellar wall, a sack over his head, and buried right there.

OLIVIER. Clear the courtyards gradually.

(*He looks at his pocket watch.*)

At nine o'clock they must be cleared. The outer doors will be left ajar, a cannon behind, loaded with case shot.—
But meanwhile—

(*he steps to the window*)

three picked sharpshooters over there. They must keep their eye on these windows. At once.

(*Jeronim goes.*)

OLIVIER. Look in there. What do you see?

ARON. (*softly*) Sigismund, Basilius' son. He stands by the bed and bends over the one who lies in it.

OLIVIER. Imprint his face on your memory. Take careful note of his measurements, how he is built, the color of his hair, every last thing.

ARON. His likeness goes around the countryside, a bad print, and they light candles before it as before an ikon.

OLIVIER. That's why. I need a fellow so like him that you could mistake him for the other, and one who suits me like the glove on my hand.

ARON. Why do you need his counterfeit, too, when you have him in person?

OLIVIER. He himself is not usable. —Let us go. I will personally give instructions to the three sharpshooters. Go.

(*Aron and Indrik leave.*)

PHYSICIAN. (*quietly opens the small door at the left front, enters hurriedly.*)

OLIVIER. (*sees him, points his pistol at him*)
Who goes there?

PHYSICIAN. (*raises his hands*) Give me one minute's hearing, sir! I am the king's physician.

OLIVIER. The man Sigismund is not sick, so far. Do you suppose he will need a physician in the near future? Are you a fortune-teller? —I know of you. We will find employment for you elsewhere. Report to the town command. Say I have sent you.

PHYSICIAN. I am at my proper post here. I have heard all that you have spoken.

(Folds his hands)

O Sir! Sir! Do you have any notion who it is you are
going to kill!

OLIVIER. None of your playacting. This cleric and comedian
style is abolished. A sober day has dawned over the world.

PHYSICIAN. Have you no idea in whose presence you were
standing? Have you no sense to perceive the nobleness
of this being?

OLIVIER. He is a man who stood before his judge just now.
That is the sober fact.

PHYSICIAN. Who is the judge over purity? Where has innocence its judge?

OLIVIER. I had thought, sir, you were a doctor, but I see you
are a parson. The concepts with which you operate, sir,
are done with and lie in the carrion pit. —The man stands
here before me: "Basilius and the Jesuit in there, that im-
postor, they have made you, the one your body, the other
your mind—therefore you are guilty, you are marked so
by fatality, and you shall be punished bodily, for we have
nothing to take hold of except your body." That is the
ruling of our court.

PHYSICIAN. Look over the whole world: it has nothing nobler
than what confronts us in this human being.

OLIVIER. I look on the world which produces the like of him
as on a juggler's booth at the fair.

PHYSICIAN. And the people feel it! Far and wide it makes
them go down on their knees!

OLIVIER. These very same creeping exhibitions will all be
abolished.

PHYSICIAN. The world is not ruled by iron clubs, but by the
spirit that is in him. He is a powerful man. Take care!

OLIVIER. Now you have pronounced his sentence. For this
he must be quashed, annulled, obliterated. To that end I
stand here. —For I and some others, we have sacrificed

ourselves and we take the burden of government off the people lest they become giddy.

PHYSICIAN. And you have come here for that?

(*He throws himself down before him.*)

OLIVIER. Indeed! People should rightly lie at our feet for what we have taken upon us, but we scorn that; nor shall they idolize our names, therefore we keep them secret. — Let go, sir, or I will free myself in a different manner.

(*He pushes the physician away and goes out.*)

PHYSICIAN. (*raises himself. Gradually the day breaks.*)

SIGISMUND. (*steps in through his door*)

Is that fellow gone? I saw him once before in another place, but now I have seen him for the last time.

ANTON. (*has entered behind Sigismund*)

Shall we be off? Down this way? Should I call somebody? Make signals?

SIGISMUND. (*remains standing and looks on the wall next to the door of his room; it reflects faintly the light of the morning sun.*)

The peasant had slaughtered a pig which was hung next to the door of my room, and the morning sun struck its inside which was dark, for its soul had been called away and had flown elsewhere. They are all joyful signs, but in what way I cannot explain to you.

(*He sits down.*)

VOICES. (*from outside*) Sigismund!

ANTON. (*at the window*) Now a great many of them are coming into the courtyard. They are looking up here.

(*He has opened the window, steps back.*)

SIGISMUND. (*sitting*) They will come for me, won't they? And I shall go forward and never again look back.

VOICES. (*outside*) Sigismund! Remain with us! Endure with us! Do not abandon us!

SIGISMUND. I am alone and I long to be united.

(*He rises.*)

VOICES. Sigismund! Do not abandon us!

ANTON. They behave just like the players at the comedy. These are not honest people.

SIGISMUND. I will go to the window and speak with my new made friends; they are calling me.

(*He goes slowly toward the window.*)

ANTON. (*anxious*) Better not, sir, not to the window!

PHYSICIAN. (*to himself*) Avert it, all-prevailing God!—or let my heart break and, sinking down, let me see the heaven in which I will be with him!

VOICES. Come to us, Sigismund!

SIGISMUND. (*steps to the open window. A shot is fired from the outside.*)

PHYSICIAN AND ANTON. (*see that Sigismund has been hit; they catch him in their arms and bring him into the interior of the room where they set him down on the chair.*)

ANTON. (*clenching his teeth*) Shot from down below! Doctor! These murderers! These vile assassins!

SIGISMUND. (*opens his eyes*) Quiet, Anton, I shall die shortly.

ANTON. As long as there is life, there is hope. I have heard this often. Do say something, doctor!

PHYSICIAN. (*feels Sigismund's pulse.*)

SIGISMUND. I feel far too well to hope. (*He is silent.*)

ANTON. And has our king nothing to say to us?

SIGISMUND. (*looks at the physician*) Bear witness, I was here, though no one has known me.

PHYSICIAN AND ANTON. (*kneel.*)

SIGISMUND. (*falls back, draws a deep breath and is dead.*)

CURTAIN

The manuscript was edited by Robert H. Tennenhouse. The book was designed by Richard Kinney. The text type face is Linotype Janson originally cut by Nicholas Kis about 1690 in Amsterdam. The display faces are Optima designed in 1958 by Hermann Zapf and Lydian designed by Warren Chapell in 1938.

The book is printed on Allied Paper Company's Paperback Book paper. The hardcover edition of the book is bound in Joanna Mills' Parchment Cloth and the paper edition in Riegal's Carolina Cover. Manufactured in the United States of America.

Alfred Schwarz received his M.A. and Ph.D. degrees from Harvard University (1947, 1951); he is currently professor of English at Wayne State University.

2D0225